"You're not enthused about finding the quads a baby daddy?"

Surely Chase wasn't volunteering for the position. Even if he were, in some alternate reality, it was impossible.

Mitzy returned his assessing look and replied, as innocently as possible, "If I were going to get married, cowboy, I would have done so ten years ago."

His eyes gleamed. "Funny. Me, too."

Thinking maybe they should go back inside before she did something really stupid, like kiss the smug look off his handsome face, Mitzy headed for the door.

Able to feel the heat of his masculine gaze, she tossed the words over her shoulder, "This is no joking matter, Chase."

For him, either, apparently.

* * *

TEXAS LEGENDS: THE McCABES:
Three generations and counting!

Dear Reader,

This month marks a big change for me.

There's sad news. Harlequin has stopped publishing American Romance and Western Romance, the beloved lines that have been my publishing home for many years.

The wonderful news? I have been invited to join the Harlequin Special Edition team. From here on out, you will be able to find all my stories about the beloved McCabe clan, and the other Texas families, such as the Lockharts and the Carrigans, under the fabulous Special Edition banner.

If you've never read one of my stories set in the utopian West Texas community of Laramie County, and aren't sure where to start, I invite you to visit my website at cathygillenthacker.com. There you will find a series guide and a McCabe family tree, as well as excerpts from every book, and links to my Facebook and Twitter pages. You can also read a little about me, as a person and a writer, and sample some of my recipes.

If, on the other hand, you've read my American and Western stories for years, and worry it just won't be the same—fear not. I guarantee that the Special Edition Cathy Gillen Thacker books to come will all have the same trademark romance, humor, heart, and sense of family and community, because there is just no way I can write a love story any other way.

And what is life without a lot of love?

Happy reading!

Cathy Gillen Thacker

The Texas Cowboy's Quadruplets

Cathy Gillen Thacker

Recycling programs
for this product may
not exist in your area.

978-1-335-46606-8

The Texas Cowboy's Quadruplets

Printed in U.S.A.

Cathy Gillen Thacker is married and a mother of three. She and her husband spent eighteen years in Texas and now reside in North Carolina. Her mysteries, romantic comedies and heartwarming family stories have made numerous appearances on bestseller lists, but her best reward, she says, is knowing one of her books made someone's day a little brighter. A popular Harlequin author for many years, she loves telling passionate stories with happy endings and thinks nothing beats a good romance and a hot cup of tea! You can visit Cathy's website, cathygillenthacker.com, for more information on her upcoming and previously published books, recipes, and a list of her favorite things.

Books by Cathy Gillen Thacker

Harlequin Western Romance

Texas Legends: The McCabes

The Texas Cowboy's Baby Rescue

Texas Legacies: The Lockharts

A Texas Soldier's Family
A Texas Cowboy's Christmas
The Texas Valentine Twins
Wanted: Texas Daddy
A Texas Soldier's Christmas

Visit the Author Profile page
at Harlequin.com for more titles.

Chapter One

"So," the way-too-handsome Chase McCabe drawled in a low, sexy voice, "the boot is finally on the other foot."

Mitzy Martin stared at the indomitable CEO standing on the other side of her front door, looking more rancher than businessman, in nice-fitting jeans, boots and tan Western shirt. Ignoring the sudden skittering of her heart, she heaved a dramatic sigh meant to convey just how unwelcome he was. "What's your point, cowboy?" she demanded impatiently.

Mischief gleaming in his smoky-blue eyes, Chase poked the brim of his hat back and looked her up and down in a way that made her insides flutter all the more. "Just that you've been a social worker for Laramie County Department of Children and Family Services for what...ten years now?"

Electricity sparked between them with all the danger and unpredictability of a downed power line. "Eleven,"

Mitzy corrected, doing her best to ignore the impressive amount of testosterone and take-charge attitude he exuded beneath his amiable demeanor.

And it had been slightly less than that since she had abruptly ended their engagement...

"And in all that time, my guess is, very few people have been happy to see you coming up their front walk. Now you seem to be feeling the very same disinclination," he continued with an ornery grin, angling a thumb at the center of his masculine chest, "seeing *me* at your door."

Leave him to point out the almost unbearable irony in that! Mitzy drew a breath, ignoring the considerable physical awareness that never failed to materialize between them. No matter how vigilantly she worked to avoid him.

She remained in the portal, blocking his entrance. And gave him a long level look that let him know he was *not* going to get to her...no matter how hard he tried. Even if his square jaw and chiseled features, thick, short sandy-brown hair and incredibly buff physique were permanently imprinted on her brain. "There's a difference, Chase." She smiled sweetly, tipping her head up to accommodate his six-foot-three-inch frame. "When people get to know me and realize I'm there to help, they usually become quite warm and friendly."

"Well, what do you know!" He surveyed her pleasantly in return. "That's exactly what I hope will happen between you and me. Now that we're older and wiser, that is."

Twins Bridgett and Bess Monroe, there to assist with her two-month-old quadruplets, appeared behind her. "Hey, Chase." Bridgett grinned.

"Here to talk business, I bet?" Bess added, a match-maker's gleam in her eye.

He nodded, ornery as ever. "I am."

Mitzy glared. She and Chase had crashed and burned

once—spectacularly. There was no way she was doing it again. She folded her arms in front of her militantly. "Well, I'm not."

He stepped closer, deliberately invading her personal space, inundating her with his wildly intoxicating masculine scent. "Mitzy, come on. You've been ducking my calls and messages for weeks now."

So what? She gave him her most unwelcoming glance. "I know it's hard for a carefree bachelor like you to understand, but I've been 'a little busy' since giving birth to four boys."

He shrugged right back, meeting her word for cavalier word. "Word around town is you've had *plenty* of volunteer help. Plus the high-end nannies your mother sent from Dallas."

Mitzy groaned and clapped a hand across her forehead. "Don't remind me," she muttered miserably.

The sympathy on his face matched his low, commiserating tone. "Didn't work out?"

"No," she bit out, "they didn't." Mostly because they had been even more ostentatious—and intrusive—than her mom. Telling her how things should be, instead of asking her how she *wanted* them to be. "Just like this lobbying effort on your part won't work, either."

"I know you'd rather not do business with me, Mitzy," he said, even more gently. "But at least hear me out."

Silence fell between them, as fragile as the still-shattered pieces of her heart. He rocked forward on his toes and lowered his face to hers. "I wouldn't be here if I didn't think it were crucial."

Mitzy caught her breath at the unexpected reminder of what it had been like to kiss him. Or how much the reckless side of her wanted to do so again.

Just to see…

"You could use a break," Bess pointed out.

Bridgett, who'd recently found her own happily-ever-after with Chase's older brother, Cullen, agreed. "And you may as well get this talk over with. If—" she paused heavily "—that's all it is."

That's all it could be, Mitzy told herself bluntly. Since there was no way she was opening up her heart to this impossibly sexy cowboy CEO again. "Fine." She ducked inside long enough to grab a fleece to ward off the chill of the November afternoon and hurried back outside. "You've got five minutes, Chase, and that is all!"

Five minutes wasn't much, but it was better than what he'd had in a very long time. Plus, he had promised her late father he'd take care of Mitzy, and her quadruplets, whether she wanted him to or not.

Chase followed Mitzy to the end of the porch on her Craftsman-style home, taking a moment to survey the recent changes in her. The birth of her four sons had given her five-nine body a new voluptuousness. Her thick medium brown hair was still threaded with honey-gold strands, but she'd cut it since he last saw her in town a month ago, and now it just brushed the tops of her shoulders. Her fair skin was lit with the inner glow she'd had since she was pregnant, her delicate features just as elegant as ever, and her lips soft and full and enticingly bare.

Which meant she still favored plain balm over lipstick. A fact he had always liked…

She bypassed the chain-hung swing and settled instead on a wicker chair. Acutely aware of how hard this was going to be for her to hear, he removed his hat, set it aside and took the seat kitty-corner from her.

Resisting the urge to take her small hand in his, he leaned toward her, hands knotted between his spread knees. Looked her in the eye and got straight to the point. "Word on the street is that Martin Custom Saddle is in big trouble financially."

Anger flared between them, even as her long-lashed aquamarine eyes widened in surprise. "I think—as CEO— that I would know if that was the case."

She certainly should have, Chase thought reprovingly. "Have you been there recently?"

Mitzy straightened. "I've been in touch with Buck Phillips—the chief operating officer—at least once a week."

Chase focused on the pretty pink color flooding her face. Matter-of-factly, he ascertained, "But you haven't actually been to the facility where the saddles are made."

She ignored his question. Stood, walked a short distance away, then swung back to face him. "What's your point, Chase?"

He hated to be the bad guy. In this situation, he had no choice. Gently, but firmly, he said, "You can't simultaneously run MCS—at least not the way your late father would have wished—and be Laramie County's best social worker. *And* all the while care for four infants all by your lonesome to boot. No one could."

Mitzy stalked toward him. "I'm not trying to do all that. I'm on maternity leave from the Department of Family and Child Services for the next ten months. Maybe longer. I haven't decided yet." Ignoring the seat close to him, she perched on the porch railing. "And Buck Phillips is running the business side at the saddle company, same as always."

Noting the way the dark denim hugged her slender thighs, and the swell of her breasts beneath the snug-fitting black fleece top, he rose and ambled toward her. "Are you sure about that?"

"Someone would have told me if there were issues. Financially, or otherwise."

Unless they were trying to protect her.

Her lower lip slid out in a sexy pout. "The employees there are not just personally invested in the success of the company, they're like family to me and each other."

With effort, Chase ignored the urge to kiss her. "It takes more than good intentions to run a company, Mitzy," he said quietly.

She tilted her chin at him, a myriad of emotions running riot in her pretty eyes. "You don't think I have it in me?"

He came closer and perched beside her. Bracing his hands on the rail on either side of him, he murmured, "Your father had a passion for saddle making."

"I know that."

He knew this would hurt. Still, it had to be said. "And you don't."

She gasped, indignant. Hands balled into fists at her sides, she bounded to her feet and swung on him once again. "I don't need to have that same passion. All I need to do is keep everything exactly the way it was when he was alive, and honor him by carrying on his legacy. And we—the company and all its employees—will be fine!"

Taking charge of a business was a lot more complicated than that. Clearly, though, she wasn't ready to hear that.

Help my daughter make it through the holidays, Gus Martin had said. *The first, after my death, will be the most difficult.*

And with Thanksgiving almost upon them...

Chase could see Mitzy was struggling. Even if she wouldn't admit it. He tried again, even more gently this time. "The point is, darlin', I'm interested in doing that, too."

Abruptly, Mitzy looked like she wanted to deck him.

"Like you did when you worked for my dad? Before he was forced to fire you?"

Of course she would bring up the business crisis that had precipitated the end of their engagement. Their breakup had ripped him up inside. Chase shrugged regretfully. "I admit, I was overly ambitious."

An even rosier hue flooded her high, sculpted cheeks. "You insulted him and everything he stood for with your plans to turn his artistry into a mass-manufacturing business."

Chase squinted. "I'm not sure your dad saw it that way."

You're meant for bigger things, Chase. You'll never be happy here...was what Gus had said, when he'd cut him loose.

And Mitzy's father had been right.

Then.

Chase had since had time to reevaluate and reconfigure his earlier career plan to something much more laudable and practical. But, sensing Mitzy was in no mood to hear that now, if ever, he slowly rolled to his feet. "Regardless of the way I left MCS, I learned a lot from your dad when I worked for him, Mitzy. I also built my own company, McCabe Leather Goods."

Her expression both contemptuous and resentful, she scoffed, "Yes, I know. It's the premier provider in the entire Southwest of all sorts of leather products. Everything from boots to saddles to leather interiors on pickup trucks and automobiles. And you did it by buying up lots of little entities and folding them into the one bearing your name!"

So she had been following his rise in the business world, Chase noted in satisfaction. He met her level gaze. "Every one of those business units is better off, their employees happier and more financially secure."

Her expression guarded, she raked her teeth across her lower lip. "So what does that have to do with me?"

"If your family business is in even half as much trouble as is rumored, you're going to need help getting it back on track."

She rolled her eyes skeptically. "*You're* volunteering?"

Yes, although first I was drafted. "Your dad was always good to me, even after I stopped working for him," Chase admitted, acutely aware of how much he missed Gus. And Gus's beautiful, intractable daughter.

Missed the extended family they might have been. "I'd like to repay his kindness."

Mitzy tilted her head at him, thinking. Seeming to know instinctively there was more to this than what he was letting on. Not about to tell her about the deathbed promises he had made, however, Chase waited for her to make a decision.

Finally, she swallowed, let out a soft little sigh. Wearily, she asked, "Don't you think it would be a little awkward under the circumstances?"

He could handle awkward. Hell, he could handle anything if it got him back into her life, and her into his. Because actually getting to have a sit-down with her, brief as it might be, had shown him certain things had not changed.

The sparks were still there.

His need to protect her was stronger than ever.

And as for the rest? Well, he guessed time would tell.

Although he couldn't imagine either of them ever being content to be just friends. Not after what they had once shared...

From the first time he'd laid eyes on her when they were kids, he'd known she was something special. Not just because she was smart and pretty or kinder and more inherently compassionate than anyone he'd ever met. From the very beginning, she just "got" him the way no one else ever had.

She hadn't wanted to date him. She'd preferred to be friends. So, they started there, but by the time they were in college there was no denying their sexual chemistry. One thing led to another. Before they knew it they were a couple and then engaged. He'd expected to spend his entire life with her.

Would have, if his need to tell it like it was, in business and in life, and her wariness of lasting love, hadn't gotten in the way. But both had, so…

Aware she was waiting, he shrugged with a great deal more carelessness than he felt. "We're both adults, Mitzy," he reminded her gruffly. "We can handle it." He pulled out a business card, wrote his cell phone number on the back and pressed it into her hand. "So if there is anything I can do," he said sincerely, resolved to keep his promise to Gus as well as atone for any and all mistakes he had made in the past. He paused to give her a long, steady look. "Anything at all, just pick up the phone and call."

Two days later, Chase still hadn't heard from Mitzy. So he did what he always did when he was trying to understand a woman. He went to see his little sister, Lulu, hoping she'd have the insight he lacked.

She listened to the recap of his visit while making her own special brand of honey iced tea for the McCabe family Thanksgiving celebration they were having later in the day. "You didn't even see the quadruplets?"

Funny how disappointed he was about that. He'd never been what one would call a baby person, but he'd been hoping to lay eyes on the four infants the stalwartly independent Mitzy'd had via an anonymous donor and a fertility clinic, nevertheless. Keeping his feelings to himself, he shrugged. "Kind of hard to do when she didn't even let me in the door."

His cell phone buzzed. Chase looked at the screen. Speak of the devil... Smiling, he strode a distance away. "Hey, Mitzy. What's up?"

"Are you busy?"

She sounded stressed.

"Not at all," Chase said.

Lulu grinned and shook her head, then sauntered out of the kitchen to give him privacy.

"I'm headed over to Martin Custom Saddle," Mitzy continued in the too-casual voice he knew so well. "Want to meet me there?"

Luckily, his sister's honeybee ranch was closer to town than his. "Be there in ten."

When Chase arrived, he expected her to already be inside the ten-thousand-square-foot production facility.

Instead, she was sitting in the new custom eight-passenger luxury SUV she'd been driving around town, staring at the front of the one-story rectangular terra-cotta brick building emblazoned with her father's name like she had never seen it before.

Noticing his pickup truck parking next to hers, she shook herself out of her reverie and emerged from the driver's seat. Her hair was swept up in a neat twist on the back of her head and she was wearing a burnished gold wool dress and heels that seemed more appropriate for a formal afternoon tea.

As she neared him, he saw the diamond earrings she'd received for her college graduation glittering in her ears, and caught the whiff of her citrus and floral perfume. He also saw faint shadows beneath her eyes that hadn't been there when he'd last seen her. Sensing her mother's holiday visit was already doing a number on her, he asked gently, "Everything okay?"

She squared her shoulders defensively. "Why wouldn't it be?"

He moved to stand beside her, wishing he could take her in his arms and not get chastised for trying to comfort her. "You look tired, I guess. A little on edge."

She flashed a wry, self-effacing smile and led the way toward the sprawling brick building. "Guilty—to all."

He moved swiftly to catch up with her and fell in step beside her, adjusting his strides to hers. He tucked his hands in the pockets of his jeans. Figuring the very least he could do was be a sounding board for her, asked kindly, "Babies giving you a hard time?" Maybe if she would actually allow him to assist her in some way, the way her dad had privately wanted, he would actually get to see them.

"No. My four boys are sweet as ever." Mitzy sighed. Her eyes took on a turbulent sheen. "It's the rest of my family that's putting me through the ringer."

The idea of rescuing her was a lot more appealing— on a soul-deep level—than it probably should have been. "Judith?"

Her lower lip slid out in a delectable pout. "She and Walter—"

Her mom's fifth husband, Chase recalled.

"—arrived in time for dinner last night. Along with four nannies."

Four again. Wow. But then that was Judith. She never did anything on the down low when the completely spectacular was possible. "One for each baby," he guessed, noting how the sunlight brought out the honey-gold highlights in her hair.

"Right." Mitzy paused to punch in the security code.

Failed. Then, releasing a frustrated sigh, she looked at her phone and tried again. This time the light turned green.

She pushed open the door and, together, they walked on in.

He caught a whiff of her flowery shampoo as she sauntered beside him. His body reacted, way too fast. Ignoring the pressure behind his fly, he asked, "You're not happy about that?"

Oblivious to the desire welling up inside him, Mitzy waved a dismissive hand and continued to look around as if she had never seen the place. Which was ludicrous. She'd been there frequently as a kid. When he briefly worked there, too. And in all this time nothing had really changed. There were a couple of offices and a break room near the front door. The rest was comprised of the twenty-nine different workstations needed to handcraft the custom leather saddles.

It smelled the same, too. Like leather and dye and industrial-strength cleaner.

Aware she hadn't answered him yet, he turned back to her again. Even in the fluorescent lighting near the door, he could see she was pale.

"This set of nannies is fine." She looked over her shoulder at him, as she walked over to the main panel and switched on the rest of the lights in the facility. "I mean, they're warm and gentle, not stern and impersonal like the first group she brought with her. And they're just going to be here for the holiday weekend. They'll all be leaving Sunday afternoon."

Chase studied her, befuddled over what was really bothering her. "Then what's the problem?" he asked.

The problem, Mitzy thought, was that she should have come back here way before now. Instead, she'd neglected to do so, figuring time and the birth of her children would ease her grief.

They had.

And they hadn't.

Because being here at the warehouse-like workshop that her father had built over the course of forty-five years, in the very place that held so many bittersweet memories for her, was like a punch square in the solar plexus. Making her entire chest hurt to the point that it was hard to breathe. As images of her larger-than-life dad striding through the facility flashed in her brain, she remembered how he had called out to everyone, stopped to admire the workmanship even as he gently added suggestions for making the final product better. How he had charmed the customers and cared for his employees with the same loving familial attitude he exhibited toward her.

With a disgruntled sigh, she also recalled the day he and Chase had gotten into it right in the middle of the shop, their voices rising. How her dad had been forced to do what he had never done in his entire business life— fire someone outright. How furious Chase had looked as he had sworn he was quitting anyway and stomped out.

And most of all, she remembered how frail her dad had been, his body ravaged from multiple surgeries and rounds of chemotherapy, the last time he had been able to walk through here. How he'd still kept up the cheerful attitude, even as he had been forced to lean on her for strength.

Her dad had been incredibly strong to the very end.

Just as she needed to be strong now.

Abruptly, Mitzy became aware that Chase was still watching her, ever so patiently waiting for her to confide in him what was really going on with her and her mother.

Telling herself there was no need to lean on his strong,

broad shoulders, she drew a deep invigorating breath, said finally, "It's just the usual stuff."

He strode closer. Clad in a pine-green brushed cotton shirt, jeans and dark brown custom boots, he looked sexy and totally at ease. "Judith still doesn't like the fact you're a social worker?"

"Correct."

He stopped just short of her and gave her the slow, thorough once-over. "I'm guessing there's more."

His soft, husky baritone sent shivers ghosting over her skin, but Mitzy stiffened her resolve, in a valiant attempt not to lose herself in his potent masculine allure. There was too much water under the bridge between the two of them, after all, and getting swept up again by passion would not be in either of their best interests.

Still avoiding her dad's private office, she moved through the shop, surveying the various workstations, finding that everything looked the same as she recalled.

Chase moved with her. "She also doesn't like me living here in Laramie, now that Dad's gone."

"She wants you back in Dallas?"

Mitzy suppressed a groan. "Permanently." Coming to the rear of the building, she stepped out onto the covered patio, where employees often took their lunch breaks.

Chase rubbed the flat of his hand beneath his jaw. "That's not so surprising, is it? Now that you've had children and made her and Walter grandparents?"

Mitzy perched on the edge of a picnic table and took in a breath of the bracing November air. "I can't go back to Dallas, Chase." She rubbed the toe of her Italian pump across the cement floor. "I never belonged there. For so many reasons, Laramie has always been my home."

Chase settled next to her, his arms crossed in front of his chest. "Me, too." He slanted a commiserating look at her. "Even when I lived away from here, I always knew I'd come back eventually."

In that sense, she and Chase were the same.

Maybe always would be.

It was too bad so many other things kept them apart. Their attitudes about business, and the role it played in a person's private life, paramount among them. He hadn't been able to understand that disrespecting her father had in turn disrespected her. And instead had insisted that she should have defended his right to speak his mind to whomever he chose. He'd also felt that, as his potential wife, she should have sided with him on principle! Even though he was clearly wrong!

When they couldn't come to terms about that, he had wanted to pretend as if their quarrel had never happened, and simply move on. She couldn't because she knew, as a social worker, that ignoring problems did not make them go away, it made them fester. A lasting relationship required a lot more than friendship, amusing repartee and incredible, skillful lovemaking. It required being on the same page—about everything important—and she and Chase weren't. And weren't going to be.

Heartbroken, she did the responsible thing and called off their engagement. Even as a tiny part of her wistfully hoped they might still find a way to meet each other halfway and work things out.

Instead, Chase had tersely agreed a split was probably for the best. Since she wasn't giving him what he needed, either. And there was no reason for them to get married, if they were only going to get divorced down the road.

And that had been that. Until now.

Aware he was waiting for her to go on, Mitzy continued cavalierly, "And of course, Judith's not happy about the whole 'single mother via artificial means' business. She would have much preferred I did things the old-fashioned way." With even Chase as her baby daddy, instead of some anonymous donor. "But since I didn't choose the more traditional route, she at least wants me to provide them with a proper father, to grow up with."

He looked down at their perfectly aligned thighs. Though an inch and two layers of fabric separated their limbs, she could still feel the warmth exuded between them. And knew he could, too.

His glance returned to hers. Stayed in a way that had her heartbeat increasing.

"You're not enthused about finding the quads a baby daddy?"

Surely he wasn't volunteering for the position?

Was he?

And even if he were, in some alternate reality, it was impossible.

She returned his assessing look. Stood, and replied, as matter-of-fact as possible, "If I were going to get married, cowboy, I would have done so ten years ago."

His eyes gleamed. "Funny. Me, too."

Thinking maybe they should go back inside, before she did something really stupid, like kiss the smug look off his handsome face, Mitzy headed for the door.

Able to feel the heat of his smoldering gaze, she tossed the words over her shoulder. "This is no joking matter, Chase."

For him, either, apparently.

He sobered, the heartbreak of the past dragging them back to the troubled confines of the present. They crossed the threshold. "I gather you asked me to come here to talk about business," he prodded.

Not sure where or even how to begin, Mitzy nodded. She might not want to turn to her ex, but he had the expertise and the dispassionate outsider's view that she desperately needed. "I did."

He looked her in the eye with a sincerity and warmth she found disquieting. "What can I do to help?"

"I went online and read some reviews of our saddles after you and I talked. They weren't as good as usual."

He hooked his thumbs through the belt loops on either side of his fly. "I'm aware. I've been reading them, too."

Guilt welled up inside her. She'd promised her dad she would take care of things. She hadn't. Thus far, anyway. That was about to change. Deliberately, she continued, "Which got me to wondering what's going on."

"Have you talked to any of the Martin Custom Saddle employees?"

She shook her head. "I wanted to come in and look around first. And the perfect time for that is today since it's Thanksgiving, and no one is slated to be working."

"And I'm here to...?"

She led him toward the front of the facility again, where production of the saddles began, her shoulder briefly nudging his bicep in the process. "Look around," she said, working to keep a more circumspect physical distance. "See if anything jumps out as a potential problem."

The first was apparently easy for him to spot. "This leather isn't top grade." He moved to another workstation. "The oils and dyes they're using aren't top quality, either."

She frowned, alarm causing her pulse to flutter. "You're sure about that?"

"Positive." His gaze narrowed. "But you don't have to take my word on that. You can look up the reputation of these suppliers yourself."

Mitzy rubbed the tense muscles of her forehead.

Chase squinted down at her. "I don't recall your father ever skimping on materials."

Mitzy winced. Admitting miserably, "He didn't."

His brows furrowed. "And you didn't order it?"

"No." Heaven's no!

His expression remained maddeningly inscrutable. "Any idea when the change might have been made?"

Her throat constricting, she headed for her dad's private office, thinking a clue as to why this all happened might be there. "I don't know." Hoarsely, she admitted, "I haven't been here since Dad died last May."

And as CEO, she should have been. Frequently. No matter how difficult or gut-wrenching she found it.

Silently berating herself for her inexcusable lapse in judgment, she slogged past the door that had always stayed open. Flipped on the lights. Saw her dad's worn denim jacket slung over the back of his chair. A box of his favorite mints sitting open on the desk. The World's Greatest Dad coffee mug she had made for him in elementary school sitting there, next to his calendar, clean and ready to be filled.

For a moment, it was almost as if her father had just stepped out for a spell. And would come striding back in, larger than life, at any second.

A sob caught in her throat, as she realized just how much she wanted that to happen.

An anguished cry left her mouth.

And then the grief and tears she'd been holding back came pouring out in a harsh, wrenching torrent.

The next thing she knew, Chase's arms were wrapped around her. He pulled her close as even more tears flowed and her slender body shook with sobs. She clung to him and he held her until the worst of the storm passed. And for one sweet moment, time really did stand still. There'd been no decade apart. No heartbreaking end to their engagement. No years of them pretending each other didn't exist. No years of not speaking.

There was only him and her, and her overwhelming need for comfort and the urge to lean on his incredible strength.

The surprising yearning to kiss him *one last time*.

So she lifted her head, and did.

Though it was supposed to be the goodbye kiss she had never given him, the final denouement in their ill-fated relationship, the brief caress quickly turned into something else entirely.

A reminder of all they had shared that was at once passionate and tender, sweet and loving, as well as a jarring testament of all they had given up.

And that, too, was more than she could bear on this very emotional day.

She and Chase had let each other down and crushed each other's hopes and dreams once. She'd be a fool to venture down the same path and hope for a different result.

Hand pressed against his chest, she tore her mouth from his and pushed him away. "No," she gasped, common sense returning with reassuring speed. It didn't matter how much she was hurting or how alone she felt.

She looked Chase in the eye. "There's no way in hell we're getting involved again!"

Chapter Two

Mitzy half expected Chase to argue with her. Try to persuade her otherwise, as he had during the days immediately following their breakup, years ago. Instead, he stood there, watchful, patient, infuriatingly silent. His implacable calm—in the wake of her complete emotional upheaval—leaving her even more on edge. Finally, he said, "You're right. We have more important issues to address right now."

What was more important than where the two of them went from here? If not straight into bed? "Like what?" Mitzy asked, wishing he didn't look so big and strong and completely irresistible.

He lounged against the wall, arms folded in front of him. "The fate of your dad's company."

Needing some distance between them, Mitzy walked around her dad's desk, then stood facing him with her hands hooked over the back of the chair. She gestured at the dust gathering everywhere she looked. "Obviously, I need to cowgirl up and get it back on track."

He nodded seriously, then warned, "Before you can do that, however, you're going to have to assess the depth of the damage."

His sexy baritone kindled new heat inside her. Aware he was watching her, gauging her reactions as carefully as she was measuring his, she tilted her chin. "You think there's more?"

"There usually is."

She inhaled deeply. Breathed out slowly. And tried not to panic considering what else she hadn't been aware of and didn't yet know.

"You're speaking of some of the small companies you've purchased and turned around," she guessed.

He nodded.

Before he could say more, a loud knock sounded on the outer door of the facility. Mitzy looked at Chase. "Expecting anyone?"

"No. You?"

With a mystified shake of her head, Mitzy crossed the cement facility floor. Her sixty-seven-year-old stepfather was standing on the other side, in the usual expensive sport coat, slacks and button-down. His thick silver hair was as neatly combed as always, his eyes warm and assessing behind the silver-rimmed glasses.

"Your mother sent me to check on you," Walter Fiedler said. "She was worried about you being here alone, but—" his glance took in Mitzy's just-kissed state and moved to Chase "—I guess she needn't have been. Hello, Chase." He extended his hand.

Chase stepped up with his usual masculine grace. "Walter."

"Good to see you."

"Likewise."

The two men exchanged polite smiles. An awkward silence fell.

Walter turned back to Mitzy. "I don't mean to pressure you, dear, but I think your mother's feelings are a
little hurt by the way you disappeared so soon after we
arrived. So if you could wrap this up…and come back to
the house soon…?"

Inundated by guilt, Mitzy said, "I'll be right there, I
promise."

The older gentleman nodded in approval, then turned
back to Chase. "Will you be joining us for Thanksgiving
dinner? Judith's cooking all of Mitzy's favorites."

It wasn't such a far-fetched assumption to make, given
the two men had initially met at a Thanksgiving dinner,
hosted by her mom, years before. Before Mitzy could decline on Chase's behalf, a spark of mischief lit his eyes.
"What time?" he asked genially.

"Two o'clock."

"Consider me in, then."

"Splendid." Walter opened the door. "See you shortly."
He headed back to his Bentley.

Mitzy turned back to her ex. Another silence fell, this
one more fraught with tension than the last. She wasn't
sure she wanted to know why he had just accepted an invitation that would have them spending even more potentially awkward time together. Unless it was to get under her
skin. A feat that he had always been able to do extremely
well. "You really don't have to feel beholden to attend."

He shrugged, once again about as movable as a boul-
der. "I'm not."

Her nipples pearled under the hot male intensity of his
gaze. "Surely, you have a McCabe family function."

He hovered closer, apparently done talking business—
for the moment, anyway. "At eight this evening. Two of my
brothers are working today, so my mom pushed our holiday gathering back until later. But if you'd rather not have

me there to act as a buffer between you and your mother, I'd completely understand."

How well he knew her. And Judith.

She studied him, tamping down the whisper of long-suppressed desire, and the notion they might ever make love again. "You'd really put yourself in the line of fire?" she asked, emotions in turmoil.

He tipped his head at her. "For you, darlin'?" He winked. "I'd even put on that sport coat and tie I've got in the back of my truck."

Mitzy had almost forgotten how turned on she got by this inherently gallant side of him and it reinforced what she had to do. "How about, then," she suggested brazenly, "we take it one step further…"

Chase had not seen Judith since he and Mitzy had broken up. He wasn't surprised to see the petite dynamo hadn't changed. Except to get thinner and blonder and even more elegant than she had been then.

"You're doing *what*?" the older woman gaped, after a brief explanation had been made.

"Going to work together to find closure," Mitzy repeated. She lifted a hand in traffic-cop fashion. "I know it sounds really basic, and in a sense it is, Mother, but the truth is Chase and I never really ended our engagement in a proper—or healthy—manner. And that lapse has kept us both from moving on the way we should."

Chase knew that to be true for him.

He'd never gotten over losing Mitzy.

It was a shock to hear her admit it so openly, though.

"As a social worker, I should have realized this a whole lot sooner," Mitzy opined, taking Chase by the hand, and leading him all the way into her cozy but well-equipped kitchen. She gestured for him to take a stool at the island, next to Walter, then sat down beside him. "But I didn't and now that I have, I want to do something about it."

"Mmm-hmm." Judith looked up from the mushroom tartlet canapés she was arranging on a silver tray.

Like Mitzy, she was dressed in a chic dress and heels. A strand of diamonds glittered at her neck.

Judith smoothed a hand over her pristine white chef's apron. "And how long is this going to take?"

Mitzy paused, seeming to be taken aback by the inquiry. "Um. I'm not sure." She looked at Chase as if waiting to be rescued again. "At least...?"

"Through the holidays," he decided.

That would give him plenty of time to figure out what that incredible kiss they'd shared earlier meant. Was she still, as it had seemed, as turned on by him as he was by her? Still privately wishing they'd never broken up. Or trying to prove to them both that it really was over between them. Romantically, anyway.

Judith exchanged a look of concern with her husband. "And then what?" she asked.

Mitzy shrugged. "We say goodbye."

Or not, Chase thought, figuring that could be negotiated, too. "When did you conclude all of this?" Judith asked.

Pink color swept into Mitzy's high sculpted cheeks. "Chase stopped by to see me a few days ago. And I, ah, I guess I started putting it all together. Today, I realized I should start following the advice I give my social work clients, and work though the residual emotions so I can move on."

"And, of course," Chase added sincerely, "I want to do that, too." More than Mitzy knew.

In fact, he had wanted to help her for months now. But

worrying his presence would make her grieving worse, he had stayed away.

"Why didn't you tell me about any of this?" Judith asked.

Mitzy rose and went to pour glasses of chilled sparkling water for everyone, handing the elders theirs first. "Because I knew you'd probably think it was all unnecessary and wouldn't approve." As she turned to hand Chase his, their fingers brushed. A jolt of heat went through him.

Mitzy's smile was fixed as she slid back onto a high-backed stool, this time being very careful not to touch him in any way. "And I didn't want to ruin your holiday. But since Walter found us together and the secret is out—" she turned to give Chase a bolstering glance "—Chase and I figured we might as well come clean. So you wouldn't have to go to all the trouble of fixing me up with anyone else."

Fixing her up? Chase's gut tightened with jealousy. Mitzy had said her mother wanted her married. She hadn't said anything about any matchmaking! But of course, it made sense. This was why she wanted him here. Not just for closure. Which, he figured was real. But to be a detriment to her mother's plans.

"I see." Judith's eyes gleamed knowingly.

She was on to Mitzy, too.

The soft sound of a baby crying had Mitzy heading for the stairs. "I'm going to see if the nannies need any help," she said.

Judith turned to check on the turkey roasting in the oven, then faced off with Chase yet again. "I'm not sure how I feel about any of this," she said.

Chase wasn't, either, if all it was, was a means to the end of him and Mitzy.

"Maybe we should let the young people figure it out for themselves, sweetheart," Walter said.

"I can't." Judith continued, "You broke my daughter's heart once."

Chase didn't mind accepting blame where it was due but he wasn't about to shoulder all of it. "I think a more apt description was that we broke each other's hearts," he clarified gruffly.

Judith paused. In the awkward silence that fell, Chase could see Mitzy's mother mentally going down the laundry list of all his faults.

As expected, she tried once again to dissuade him.

"The point is, Chase, Mitzy deserves more than you can give her."

Chase knew he'd been far too focused on fulfilling his ambition then, to the detriment of all else. He nodded. "She deserves more than I did give her, ten years ago."

Judith's gaze narrowed. "I'm not just talking about time and attention, although there is that. I'm talking about the financial aspect, too."

Obviously, although his ex had kept up with his accomplishments, her mother had not.

Chase was still trying to figure out how to disclose his greatly improved status, without sounding like a braggart, when Mitzy came back into the kitchen, an infant in a BabyBjörn carrier, snuggled against her chest. To Chase's frustration, the infant's face was turned away from him, so all he could see was the outline of the baby boy's sturdy little body, encased in the canvas carrier, and the blue-and-white knit cap covering his head.

Clearly, she'd overheard enough of the conversation to know what was going on. "Can we please not talk about money today?" Mitzy swayed back and forth, gently lulling the child. A more natural mother had never been made, Chase thought admiringly. "Besides, haven't you heard,

Mother?" Mitzy added wearily. "Chase is wealthy in his own right now."

Her spine stiff with indignation, Judith gave the gravy another stir. "Darling, there's wealthy. And then there's *wealthy*."

Mitzy made a face. She walked farther away from the trio. Giving him an even better view of her enticing backside and spectacular legs.

Judith continued brightly, "The men I have lined up for you to meet at the quadruplets' debut have fortunes on par with Walter's."

Only one problem with that, Chase thought, as he swept another wave of unwanted jealousy aside. Money and/or influence had never been what Judith's daughter wanted. That had been *his* ambition.

"Your mother could have a point," Chase said, playing against Mitzy's widely stated values.

She met his eyes.

New sparks flew.

He shrugged affably. "The fifty-million-dollar company I started is probably nothing compared to what those dudes likely inherited." And if their blood was as blue as he imagined, they probably did nothing to earn...

Mitzy shot him a droll look and glided nearer, giving him another tantalizing but maddeningly incomplete glimpse of just one of her four sons.

What was it going to take to get an introduction?

Although he knew very well why she wasn't showing him her boys.

She was trying to keep at least some boundaries erected between them.

"I want more than money from anyone I'm involved with," Mitzy said sternly.

Chase was glad to hear that. It meant Mitzy was as

deeply romantic as she had once been before practicality trumped all and she had decided to have her babies the new-fashioned way. Sans intimacy of any kind.

"Why do you assume that just because a man is rich he's somehow not worth having?" Judith demanded, taking the potatoes off the stove to drain.

Chase noted the grinning Walter seemed to agree with Judith that he was very much worth having.

Mitzy continued her gentle waltz about the kitchen. "I don't know, Mother." She bent to kiss her baby's head, then cast a chastising glance over her shoulder. "Maybe your second, third and fourth husbands might have something to do with it?"

Chase knew Mitzy's previous stepfathers had all been emotionally remote and/or neglectful, at best, often viewing Mitzy as a nuisance. Luckily, she'd had Gus, and her time in Laramie to counter that.

"Exactly why I promptly divorced them after only a year or two," Judith huffed, handing over a bottle of wine for her husband to open. "They weren't the right person for me to be married to."

"But they were increasingly wealthy," Mitzy pointed out as Walter worked off the cork.

"Well, of course." Judith refused to apologize for that as she passed the canapés around. "I wasn't going to fall for anyone who guaranteed us downward mobility!" She paused to put the tray aside then grasped Mitzy by the shoulders. "Listen to me, darling, it is just as easy to fall in love with a wealthy man as it is to fall in love with a poor one. The difference is a truly wealthy man has so many more ways to make you happy! And if you need an example of that—" Judith let go of Mitzy and went to kiss her fifth husband on the cheek "—you need to look no further than my darling Walter."

Chase wanted to disagree with that, but couldn't. Not entirely, anyway. It was a heck of a lot easier to be happy if you didn't have to worry about putting food on the table or a roof over your head.

Mitzy frowned. "I'm not disputing the fact that Walter is wonderful, Mother, or always has been." She sent Walter an affectionate smile, which he returned. "But it's not his money or his talent with investing that makes him so exceptional. It's his kind heart and generosity."

Judith took the turkey out of the oven and set it on the back of the six-burner stove. "You think Chase has your best interests at heart?"

Mitzy paused, a little too long for his comfort. Which meant he had a lot of work to do to get their relationship back on an even keel.

"Yes. Of course," Mitzy said finally. She added as a caveat, "Now, anyway."

Still managing the meal prep with a former chef and caterer's ease, Judith turned to him with a raised brow. "I assume you'll attest to the same?"

"Absolutely." Chase held Mitzy's pretty aquamarine eyes. If the past few days had taught him anything, it was that he wanted a fresh start with his ex-fiancée. And that yearning had nothing to do with any secret deathbed promise he'd made to Gus.

"Then prove it." Judith threw down the gauntlet with customary flair. "Use your clout within the industry to find a buyer for Martin Custom Saddle, or purchase it yourself, so Mitzy can finally be free of the company that's ruined our family from the get-go. And then help my daughter understand that much as she might *want* to be, she's not a superwoman."

Maybe not in Judith's view, Chase thought wistfully. But in his, she was pretty darn close. For a mortal, anyway.

"Mother," Mitzy groaned, putting one hand to her head.

Ignoring the entreaty, Judith carried on. "So if she wants her babies to have the fabulous first Christmas they deserve, she needs to put off all this closure business..."

Like hell they would, Chase thought.

"...say goodbye to you. Leave Laramie for good. And come and live with us in Dallas, ASAP."

"Thanks for coming by," Mitzy told Chase at eight o'clock Sunday evening. She ushered him inside the Craftsman-style bungalow she had inherited from her father. As Chase walked in, he took a moment to look around.

Many changes had been made since Gus had passed. Walls in the living area had been opened up. The interior had been painted a welcoming ivory, which attracted tons of sunlight and contrasted nicely with the newly refinished pine floors. Plantation shutters replaced the dated drapes, comfortable neutral furniture had been brought in to replace the old faux leather pieces. And of course the kitchen, family room and dining area between, where they had spent most of Thursday, had all been redone and redecorated with the same classic understated elegance for which Mitzy was known.

Only one room downstairs appeared to have been left untouched, he had noted the other day. Gus's dark, paneled study. And most of the time, Mitzy left that door closed.

Chase turned his attention back to Mitzy. She was dressed in figure-hugging gray yoga pants and a long-sleeve white T that did equally nice things for her lush breasts. The need to haul her into his arms and make love to her intensifying, he lifted his gaze back to her face. "You said you needed to see me?"

"That's right, I did." Mitzy took his jacket and hung it in the coat closet. Then led him toward her father's old study, where it seemed she had set up quite an organizing operation.

"What's all this?" Chase looked at the four large bulletin boards set up on easels around the room.

One held sticky notes of calls needing to be made to various colleagues at the DCFS office. The next a schedule of baby-wrangling volunteers for the week. A third, a list of Christmas errands and chores to be done. The fourth was blank except for the initials MCS, the family saddle company.

A glimmer of ambition lit her pretty eyes. "I think of it as my war room."

He pointed to the holiday to-do list, slanting her a concerned glance. She had at least one activity slated for every day. "You'll definitely need a battle plan to get this all done. Even without four babies."

Mitzy's lips set in a deliciously kissable moue. "Don't start. You'll sound like Mother."

Brought up short by the comparison, Chase lifted a staying hand. "Sorry," he said brusquely. After that tension-filled Thanksgiving dinner he was pretty sure that Mitzy lamented him impulsively agreeing to attend, that was the last thing either of them wanted. Him criticizing or undermining her at every turn, even in jest. "You deserve my unbridled support," he said soberly. "I'm here because I plan to give it."

Their eyes met. Another shimmer of heated desire sizzled between them. "Thank you," Mitzy choked out emotionally. "I appreciate that." Her cheeks pinkening, Mitzy swept a hand through her tousled hair. Shoving it away from her face, she went on with difficulty, "I asked you to come over tonight because I wanted to apologize for what happened on Thursday. It was…" She paused, clearly at a loss for words.

Chase guessed at what she was about to say. "One of the most stilted holiday meals either of us have ever had?"

Mitzy laughed ruefully. As did he.

Resisting the urge to pull her into his arms, Chase continued with a shrug, "The food was amazing, though."

"Still, I should have known better than to let Mother have access to you. She's never forgiven either of us for canceling our wedding at the last minute. Even if it was the right decision."

Maybe at the time. Now, seeing Mitzy again, kissing her and feeling those emotions rekindle, Chase was not so sure.

He also knew his ex-fiancée was a "one step at a time" person. He couldn't rush her into anything.

She reached over to turn on the woefully outdated desktop computer located in the center of the desk. "So, as far as Mother's third degree about the scope and success of your business. Never mind her wild idea about you finding a buyer for MCS..."

Or purchasing it myself, Chase added silently.

Mitzy winced as the computer slowly—and noisily—booted up. "Or talking me into moving back to Dallas in time for the holidays, in exchange for her blessing on our monthlong closure process...?"

Sensing she needed her space, he moved to the overfilled bookcases. "You'd prefer I earn it some other way."

Mitzy made a seesawing motion. "I'm not really sure that's possible," she admitted, tossing a candid glance his way, "even if you were to do everything Mother asked. As you might have noticed, the women in my family can hold a grudge."

He sure as heck had.

Mitzy lifted her chin. Totally serious now. "Still, I'd like to call a permanent truce between the two of us."

Gratitude welled.

He ambled toward her. "I'd like that, too, darlin'." He paused on the other side of the desk. Noted the quick, excited jump in her pulse and decided to just go for it. "So does this mean you want to start seeing me again instead of just working on 'closure'?"

Her smile faded. She arched a censuring brow. "I'm seeing you now."

He shook his head and moved around to stand next to her. "Seeing you as in *dating* you." He tucked an errant strand of hair behind her ear. "The sparks are still there, Mitzy." Evidenced anew by the erratic nature of her breathing. "We proved that the other day."

With a smile, she danced away. "Actually, I was thinking we might try something else while we work our way out of the animosity that has plagued us for the past decade." She moved one of her easels slightly, before spinning back to him. "Something more platonic and casual." She met his level gaze with familiar stubbornness. "Like friendship."

Which was nothing remotely close to what he wanted.

Sifting through his disappointment, Chase took a moment to consider.

In the past, he would have told her it was his way or the highway. She would have said the same to him. That approach had never worked. So if he wanted to pursue any kind of relationship with her, he would have to do more than simply pick up where they had left off. He would have to revise their way of dealing with each other into something that would weather hardship and stand the test of time.

"Okay," he said, willing to give this friendship thing a whirl, at least for now. Anything to avoid the permanent "closure" she'd been talking about. "I'll give it a try."

"Good." She smiled, mirroring his enthusiastic tone. "Because I need your help."

"Putting up Christmas decorations?"

So far, she'd done absolutely nothing on that score. Which was unlike her. Usually, Mitzy went to get a tree and started hauling out the decorations the day after Thanksgiving.

Amazing, how easily he could envision himself helping her decorate for the holidays. When he was on his own, it wasn't really his thing. Although he was always around to help his parents and his sibs.

She tilted her head, as used to denying herself what she wanted as he was in going after it no holds barred. Openly curious, she queried, "Are you volunteering?"

Aware he'd do anything that might bring them closer, Chase nodded. "I am."

"Well," she said, mischief sparkling, "I could use someone to help with the heavy lifting."

Given how fit she was, he doubted she really needed it. "Want" was something else entirely, however. Bolstered by the idea she might privately yearn for more with him, too, he aimed a thumb at the center of his chest. "Then I'm your man."

Mitzy raked her teeth across the soft lusciousness of her lower lip. "I could also use your help with a few other things, as well…"

Though so far he'd had only a brief, blocked glimpse of one of her four infants, it stunned him to realize how much he wanted to meet them and help her with them, too. "The babies?" he asked eagerly.

She shook her head. Her gaze darkened worriedly. "With figuring out what's really been going on at MCS."

Chapter Three

Mitzy wasn't sure how Chase would take her request. Especially after the "conditions" her mother had thrown out. His long pause indicated she had been right to worry. She could feel him sizing her up, trying to figure out the exact nature of her innermost feelings about him. When she didn't really know herself.

All she knew for certain was that she had appreciated his kindness. Enjoyed kissing him—way too much! And that she wanted the cold war between them to end, so she wouldn't have to keep going out of her way to duck his sexy presence, now that he was living back in Laramie.

He continued to study her wordlessly.

She jerked in a breath, wary of inadvertently revealing too much. "That is why you initially came to see me, correct? To lend aid in any way I needed?"

In the kitchen, an "end of cycle" bell sounded.

"Yes." His mood was suddenly all business.

Mitzy glanced at her watch. The boys would be waking

soon for their next feeding. It was time to get a move on. Wishing she weren't quite so aware of his presence, she retreated into scrupulous politeness. "Unlike my mother, I'm not asking you to find a buyer for MSC." She pivoted and headed for the kitchen.

Chase stood to the left of her, watching as she opened the dishwasher, pulled out two dozen newly sterilized baby bottles as well as the basket of sterilized nipples and caps, then set them all on the counter.

The way he looked at her then—as if he was thinking what it might be like to make love to her again—sent tremors of aching need tumbling through her.

"And if I could find a buyer?" he asked.

Mitzy shook her head. Aware that every time she got near him her heart beat faster, her senses got sharper and the romantic disappointment she'd felt since their breakup became more acute. All factors, she knew, that made her ripe for a renewed affair. And that could be disastrous, given the fact he was still all business. And she was…now more than ever…all family.

Yes, they still had sparks. And an amazing rapport.

Yes, she was incredibly attracted to him.

And even still enjoyed spending time with him.

But she did not want to end up in the same place they'd been before, with him choosing to pursue a financial bottom line over her feelings, or those she loved.

She couldn't be with someone who had once felt that semiautomation of the MCS saddle-making process had been the way to go, even if it disrespected her father's artistry and cost some of their beloved employees their jobs.

She could, however, rely on his expertise in the leather business to help get MCS back on track. And she knew her late father would very much approve of that!

Deciding she had gotten lost in his mesmerizing gaze

for far too long, she went to the pantry and emerged with a gallon of purified water and a new can of powdered infant formula.

Promising herself she was not going to let herself fall victim to the attraction simmering between them, she forced her gaze back to the rugged contours of his face. "I could never let the company go." She set both items on the counter. "Not when I promised my father I would always take care of it."

His eyes narrowed skeptically. "Did Gus want you to run it personally?"

She made a show of opening both containers, then went down the row, adding one scoop of powdered mix to each bottle. "It's why Dad left it to me, and made me the CEO before he died."

"Gus never discussed you selling MCS if it became too much?"

Mitzy flushed. "Well, yes." She bent her head and added purified water to each bottle, too. "When it became clear my dad's cancer was terminal and he didn't have long to live, he and I talked about the possibility."

"And?" Moving closer, he flashed her an encouraging smile.

Mitzy handed Chase the bottle and gestured for him to continue. While he did, she topped them off with nipple, plastic screw cap and protective cover.

"What did your dad say to you?" he prodded.

"That I could sell if I wanted. But I didn't want to."

Chase paused. He slanted her a perplexed look. "Why not?"

"Because his custom saddle company was his baby as much as I was! He started it from scratch in a one-room operation and, over the years, built it into a multimillion-dollar operation with twenty-nine employees. The quality of the work at MCS has always been legendary. Until the last year, while I've been in charge," she admitted unhappily as she lifted the capped bottles and shook them vigorously to mix. "Which is why, more than ever, I have to get things back on track. I have to carry on his incredible legacy, not just for myself, but for my sons! And their offspring, too!"

Chase seemed to understand her need to make this more than a one- or two-generation family business. He stepped in to help with the mixing, his biceps flexing against the soft cotton of his shirt. "Have you talked to anyone at the company yet?"

Mitzy consulted her watch again, then took four of the finished bottles over and put them in the warmers. "No. It's a holiday weekend."

"But you're going to." He helped her move the rest of the prepared baby bottles into the fridge.

Mitzy nodded. Knowing communication was always key. "Eventually, yes, when I have a better idea of what's going on." Chase's shoulder brushed hers as he put the last of the formula into the fridge. "How are you planning to get the facts without talking to employees?"

Arm tingling, Mitzy stepped back. "That's where you come in. I was hoping if you looked at the company records with me, via the log-in on my dad's desktop computer, we might be able to pinpoint how and why and when everything began going wrong."

"And then what?" He turned his pensive gaze on her.

She adopted a brisk businesslike demeanor. "I'll talk privately to whoever is responsible for making some of the decisions that have lowered the quality of our saddles substantially."

He came closer. "Planning to fire them?"

She scoffed and backed up until her spine rested against

the quartz countertop. "No! These people are all family." Her heart ached at the mere idea. "I'll just make sure they understand, we'll make a course correction and that will be that."

He asked, tone matter-of-fact, "You have access to all the company records?"

Glad he was there to help her navigate the unfamiliar inner workings of the business, she said, "Every last one."

He kept his eyes locked with hers. And leaned forward close enough for her to inhale the brisk masculine scent of his aftershave lotion. "Is everything computerized?"

She ignored the comforting warmth of his body, so near to hers. Frowning, she pushed back the unwanted emotion welling up inside her. "I think so."

Concentration lines appeared at the corners of his eyes. "You're not sure." His expression remained genial, but otherwise inscrutable.

Reluctantly, Mitzy admitted, "I've never actually looked. I gave everyone the autonomy to make the decisions they felt necessary, just the way my dad did when he was first diagnosed with stage four bone cancer and began undergoing treatment."

"Which was a year ago, October."

Mitzy was surprised Chase remembered that so precisely, since he had still been living in Fort Worth at the time.

Throat tightening, she went to him and laid an entreating hand on his forearm. "The point is, Chase, when I go to them, with whatever the situation is, I want to also have the solution at the ready."

He nodded. A mixture of understanding and acceptance came into his eyes. Covering her hand with his own, he asked gently, "So what is your timetable?"

Mitzy savored the warmth and strength of him. "I want

this all wrapped up before the MCS annual Christmas party, on the twenty-second of December."

His brow furrowed. "That means we're going to have to get started with the audit right away."

Taking comfort in the fact she wasn't going to be locked in this stressful situation all on her own, Mitzy nodded. Chase might not know her as well as she had always wished, but he did know business.

She frowned as she heard the sound of a fussing baby on the monitor.

She dropped her hold on Chase and stepped back, then headed for the stairs. Remembering to add, "And one more thing, Chase. This all has to be done in secret."

Of course it did, Chase thought, as he followed Mitzy up the staircase to the second floor. Trying and failing not to admire the snug fit of her yoga pants over her gently rounded derriere. She cast him a warning look over her shoulder. "I don't want people worrying unnecessarily, Chase. Especially not during the Christmas season!"

Of course she didn't.

Just like her father hadn't wanted *her* to worry when he was sick.

I'd sell MCS to you right now, Chase, if just the idea of it weren't so upsetting to my daughter, Gus had said, from his hospital bed, that last week.

Heartsick at the way the disease had ravaged the body of his mentor, and almost father-in-law, Chase had pulled up a chair and taken Gus's frail hand in his. *Did you try talking to her?*

Yes. And she took that to mean I was giving up. My death is going to be hard enough on her as it is, and we both know it's coming, Gus had grimaced, *a heck of a lot sooner than I would like.*

Unhappily—because no good had ever come from keeping someone deliberately in the dark—Chase had guessed, *So the plan is to humor Mitzy?*

Gus had nodded. *Until the end of the fiscal year. By then, she should have realized she's not cut out for the business world, any more than I was ever meant to be a social worker. I want you to help her let MCS go, Chase... so she can move into the future, unencumbered...*

"Chase?" Mitzy came back to the nursery door, to find him barely clearing the top step. "Did you want to see the babies?"

Abruptly, he realized she had been talking to him. He'd been so lost in the poignant memory of her dad, he hadn't heard a word of what she'd said.

"Sorry." He lifted an apologetic hand. "Thinking..."

She looked stressed. "The volunteers are going to be here in another half an hour, but I don't think the boys are going to make it that long. They're usually pretty hungry upon waking."

It was easy to see why she might feel overwhelmed in the moment. He didn't know how she had made it thus far. "Not to worry. I'm here."

Glad he was there to come to their rescue in a way he hadn't been in the past, when he hadn't spent nearly enough time understanding where Mitzy was coming from or why...never mind tried to meet her halfway on anything... or persuade her to do the same with him... He hurriedly closed the distance between them and followed her into the nursery. He and Mitzy had been too young before to realize just how incredible and rare the love they had was. But they were older now, wiser. So if they ever got even half of what they'd had back, he was damn sure not going to squander it. And he wouldn't let her do so, either.

In the meantime, he'd help her—and her sons—in every way he could, as a way of making amends.

He wanted her to see she could count on him, the way her father had hoped, and more. And so could her boys.

"Wow," Chase said, as he caught his first glimpse of Mitzy's four adorable new sons.

For once, the talk around town had been right on the mark. The quadruplets were gorgeous, just like their mom, with dark hair, fair skin and big, long-lashed blue eyes. As Mitzy surveyed them, she beamed with pride. He could see why. They were just perfect. As was the nursery she had set up for them.

The four full-size white cribs were fit together in the middle of the room, like a foursquare. All were decked out in "baby boy" blue. Colorful, eye-catching mobiles were attached to each bed. The babies all wore engraved bracelets that coincided with the names written across the tops of all the side railings.

Mitzy made the introductions proudly. "This is Joe." The most social, Chase guessed, taking in the long lashes. "He is always smiling and laughing and cooing."

She moved to the next bed. "And this is Zach." Who still seemed sleepy, Chase observed, as the little one yawned. Mitzy smiled. "He's my little Zen baby. Peaceful, content, never complaining."

She moved on to the third crib, announcing proudly, "Here's Alex." The little fella had worked one arm out of his swaddling, Chase noted with admiration. And was attempting to free the other. "He's going to be my athlete," Mitzy proclaimed.

"And then—" she paused at the fourth crib "—there is Gabe." The infant was staring up at them, intent, seeming wise beyond his days. "He seems to be the most perceptive of the four," she said softly. "He's always vigilant, always aware."

Chase started to speak. Briefly, he was so overwhelmed with emotion it felt like he had a frog in his throat. Finally, he managed to say in a rusty-sounding voice, "They're amazing."

"I know." Mitzy's eyes gleamed suspiciously, too.

Chase took her in his arms, hugging her. "Congratulations, Mom," he whispered, his voice still sounding a little hoarse.

She nodded, overcome.

Hanging on to him until it became clear if this continued they would kiss, she cleared her throat. Blinking, she extricated herself and turned away. Chase could hardly blame her. The situation between them was precarious enough as it was.

Plus, the babies needed to be fed.

There would be plenty of time in the month to come for them to explore the rest of their feelings. And hopefully discover why they *shouldn't* search out closure…

Mitzy took the elastic from her wrist in one hand, captured the thick silky length of her hair with the other and secured it in a high bouncy ponytail on the back of her head.

Smiling, she pushed up the sleeves on her close-fitting T-shirt, all earth mom now. "Would you mind pushing the play button on the stereo, then starting all the mobiles? The combination helps keep them calm while I change their diapers."

"Happy to." Glad she was finally including him in this part of her life, Chase did as asked. The soothing sounds of orchestral lullabies filled the room. He edged closer, wanting to be more than a bystander. Waiting until she was done with the bottle of hand sanitizer, he then helped himself to some and asked, "Can I give you a hand?"

"You know how to do this?" Still rubbing her own hands together, disinfecting them, she shot him an astonished look, reminding him he hadn't been much for babies when they had been together.

"I helped my brother Jack with his three little ones after he lost his wife."

She handed him a couple of clean diapers, some wipes. "I remember you being in town a lot for a while after."

A long while, actually, Chase thought. "He had a nanny, too, but he needed family."

Mitzy sent him a commiserating glance. "Don't we all."

They worked in silence. Unsnapping. Diapering. Until all four boys were clean, dry and comfy.

"Now what?" Chase couldn't imagine how she faced this alone. Even for a moment. Although to her credit, all four babies were still calm. Patient.

Mitzy smiled, looking both grateful for and appreciative of his help. "We take them downstairs."

A feat that took two trips for each of them. He was looking forward to giving bottles, too. Would have, if a few members of Mitzy's volunteer army of other women hadn't arrived.

The next thing Chase knew, the two helpers were with the babies, and he and Mitzy were alone on the front porch.

She'd waved off his offer to wait while she got a jacket— probably because she wanted to keep this goodbye short— and instead stood, arms crossed in front of her chilled breasts. "So about what we were talking about earlier. I know you have your own work to do during the days." She lifted her chin to search his eyes. "Would it be possible for you to get started helping me tomorrow evening?"

The sooner he could make inroads on restoring his

friendship with Mitzy, the better. "Sure," he agreed, glad to help her in any way he could. Even if she wasn't exactly making it easy. "What time?"

She raked her teeth across her lush lower lip. Shivering harder now. "Between eight and ten?"

Chase felt the sharp urge to haul her against the warmth of his body and kiss her again. But instead, he tamped down that desire and settled for touching her hand briefly, telling himself their time would come. "I'll see you then."

Chapter Four

Mitzy's heartbeat accelerated the minute she heard the doorbell ring the following evening.

She inhaled deeply and headed for the door.

Chase was on the other side of the portal. His short sandy-brown hair clean and neatly brushed, his face closely shaven and smelling of aftershave, he was as gussied up as if they had been going on a date.

She'd spent a little time on her appearance, as well.

"Hey," she breathed, resisting the urge to bring him in close for the casual hug she gave most of her good friends. "You're right on time." Something that had almost never been true, years before, when they'd actually been a couple.

He hefted the big beautiful Christmas wreath in one hand, the oversize bag from the hardware store, bearing what appeared to be prelit evergreen garlands and red velvet holiday bows, in the other. She caught a whiff of his brisk woodsy cologne as he stepped over the threshold. He winked at her genially. "And bearing gifts."

Something he had done a lot, when they were together.

Feeling another whoosh of attraction, she took the packages that he handed her. A self-conscious flush moved from her chest up to her cheeks. "You didn't have to do this."

He shrugged affably, his gaze moving up and down the length of her. "I thought decorating the front of your home might help put you in the holiday spirit. You know," he roughly paraphrased her favorite Christmas story, "deck the halls. And mistletoe…and presents to pretty girls…"

Just being with him again made her heart skip another beat. She focused on the wispy curls springing from the open collar of his shirt. "There isn't any mistletoe here."

"Really?" He leaned closer, his warm breath whispering across her ear. "That's a shame."

She shot him a "contain yourself" look. "And there better not be any in this bag, either, cowboy."

"Sad to say." He sighed comically, holding her eyes in the rakish manner she knew so well. "There's not."

Yet, she thought, knowing him a lot better than she wished she did.

Past experience told her he would put the moves on her again.

The current sizzle of chemistry promised she would have a very hard time resisting. No matter how much she wanted to keep them from hurting each other again…

"In any case…" Ignoring the mixture of excitement and ambivalence roaring through her, she worked to get the conversation back on track. "Sorry if I've been a little glum. I don't mean to bring you or anyone else down." She took his coat and hung it in the hall closet. "But it's hard to be merry when I've got business problems on my mind."

"Hey." He curved a gentle hand over her shoulder. Understanding glowed in his gray-blue eyes. "Whatever the difficulties are," he promised in his husky baritone, "they're nothing we can't fix."

Mitzy swallowed and licked her lips. *"We?"*

Another spark lit between them. Hooking his thumbs through his belt loops, he rocked forward on the toe of his boots. Shrugged carelessly. "I said I'd help you, and I meant it."

"I appreciate it." She refused to let down her guard. "But as for the decorations..." She knew it would be a mistake to be more beholden to him than she was already going to be.

He lifted a hand before she could offer to reimburse him. "We're going to need a reason to explain why I'm suddenly coming over here evenings. Tonight, it happens to be a holiday errand slash housewarming slash hostess gift."

She wasn't surprised he had a plan. He always had a plan. It was one of the things that made being around him so reassuring. At least when she was in a situation where she needed help or yearned to feel protected. At other times...like when he'd worked for her dad at MCS...the fact he'd entertained a plan—to modernize a business that was not in need of change—had caused an undue amount of havoc. Not just for the two of them personally, but for her whole family and, in a sense, MCS, too.

Prior to that, Gus had never fired anyone.

After that, there was the fear he might do so again.

Although he never had.

Luckily, since this arrangement was going to be brief, and just between the two of them, she figured it would be okay. As long as they were careful, that was.

She led the way down the hall, into her father's old study. The one room in the house she had inherited from him that she had not changed. "So you've had questions from others about our 'relationship,' too." She led the way into the wood-paneled abode with the massive desk, built-in bookcases, leather sofa and chair. He looked as at home here as he had always been.

Sitting down at the desk, she turned on the computer.

Chase stood, hands curved over the high back of the reading chair in front of him. "Five different people today mentioned they'd heard about us keeping company again."

Mitzy waited for the antiquated system to boot up, then logged on. "I only had three. And they were just gentle inquiries."

Chase winced and revealed wryly, "Mine were more along the line of 'I better not break your heart again, or else.'"

Trying not to notice how the blue-gray fabric of his shirt nicely delineated the sculpted muscles of his chest, and brought out the stormy hue of his eyes, Mitzy wrinkled her nose at him. "Ouch."

"I told them all not to worry," he returned mildly, more confident than ever. "I won't ever do anything to hurt you again."

She knew he wouldn't mean to hurt her. He hadn't in the past, either. Just as she hadn't meant to dis him. But their differing priorities and mind-sets had caused them to do just that, anyway. Which was why she wanted to proceed cautiously. See if they could find a way to be friends again first. And then, and only then…when they could trust each other again…move on from there.

Mitzy swallowed and focused on getting into the MCS business database.

Aware he was waiting for her reaction to his contrite assertion, she said, just as penitently, "You really shouldn't have to take all the blame for that." She girded herself against the attraction simmering between them, then paused to meet his appreciative gaze. "I was as single-minded and hotheaded as you were back then."

His broad shoulders flexed. "Luckily, we've both matured."

They had. It didn't mean she was any less aware of him, though. If anything, she wanted him more than ever. And that could be a problem, given the fact they still wanted very different things in life. She wanted a laid-back small-town existence for herself and her quadruplets. He was still building his multimillion-dollar leather goods empire. Yes, he had recently bought a ranch here in Laramie County, but according to his only sister, Lulu, he also had a loft in Fort Worth, a condominium in a downtown Houston high-rise, a place on the beach in Galveston and a home in the Panhandle.

Real estate, for him, was just another investment, and a bottom-line-friendly place to stay whenever—wherever—he was doing business.

So she couldn't make too much of the fact he was back in Laramie County, when he could just as soon be gone tomorrow.

Aware that for every good thing in her life, there was also something troubling, Mitzy sighed.

Chase tilted his head, listening to the quiet in the house and the lack of sound coming from the baby monitor on the study shelf. Brow furrowing, he asked, "Where are the quads?"

Mitzy typed in another command. "Asleep in the family room in their bassinets, although for how long I don't know." She made a face. "They've been really off schedule since my mother and Walter visited."

Finally seeing what she wanted on-screen, she gestured for him to come closer. He pulled up a chair next to her and sat down.

"Where do you want to start?" he asked.

Good question, Mitzy thought, aware all over again how ill-equipped she was to be running the financial side of the business. Yet she had promised her father she would preserve the company he had built. Make sure his legacy endured. She intended to keep that vow even if it meant putting aside her usual independence and enlisting Chase's help.

"I logged on to the MCS system earlier in the day. To tell you the truth, I couldn't really figure out how we're doing, at least when it comes to the bottom line."

Chase soon saw why. Every business transaction was entered in a general document, and there was one for each day of the work year. So, they knew everything that had happened on June 1, for instance, but they didn't know how each action impacted the MCS balance sheet.

He rocked back in the chair, while Mitzy perched on the edge of the desk, to his left. "Has it always been like this?" he asked eventually, aware he still didn't know much about the financial side of MCS. During the brief time he'd worked for her dad, after he and Mitzy had become engaged, he had been focused on learning the ins and outs of working with leather, and the complex craft of saddle making.

He'd seen even then, improvements could be made. But Gus hadn't wanted to change anything, even if it would add nicely to the bottom line.

Looking back, understanding fully the hand-crafted artistry of what they did, Chase understood his mentor's point of view.

But back then, his firing, followed by Mitzy's refusal to back him up in any way, had been a bitter pill to swallow.

Pushing his disappointment away, he forced himself to

concentrate on the task at hand. "Has MCS always kept their records in such a haphazard manner?"

The fragrance of lavender-scented baby powder clung to her. Inundating him. She bit her lower lip. For a moment, surprisingly vulnerable.

Surprisingly like the woman he'd once fallen in love with.

"I think so."

He pushed aside the desire to take her in his arms and kiss her senseless.

"But you're not sure?"

Mitzy shrugged. "I never tried to look at the books until this morning. I just talked to the employees from time to time, and they said everything was fine. Which must mean that financially the company is still okay. Right?"

Not necessarily, Chase thought. But not wanting to alarm her until he knew the facts, he turned his glance away from the kissable lines of her mouth and asked, "Who is in charge of managing the financials now?"

She took a deep breath that lifted and lowered the luscious curves of her breasts. "Buck Phillips, our chief operating officer." Restless, she stood and walked away, then pivoted back to him. "And he told me he was doing all the record keeping the way my dad always did, and then figuring everything out at the end of the fiscal year. Which for us is December 31."

A hell of a way to run a business.

Mitzy blinked and came closer. "You didn't know any of this?" she asked.

Chase shook his head. As he reflected, his gaze drifted over her. Taking in the way the soft light of the study illuminated the peachy hues of her skin, and her shimmering honey-brown hair draped her shoulders.

She might not want to admit it to him, but—new mother or not—she was a very sensual woman. It was apparent in the smooth lines of her ivory V-neck cashmere sweater and the perfect fit of her skirt over her gorgeous derriere.

His body tightening, he said, "Gus never showed me the books. He and I talked mostly about craftsmanship and modernization issues."

Mitzy perched on the edge of the desk, her arms folded in front of her. Mouth sober, she guessed, "And my dad didn't want to make any changes."

"No." And Gus really should have, Chase reflected grimly. Because then Mitzy wouldn't be in such a mess.

"So what next?" she asked, stretching her long lissome legs out in front of her and crossing her ankles.

Chase was not one to hold back, especially in situations this potentially serious, but as he looked at her sweet, vulnerable expression, all he felt was an overwhelming need to protect her, the way he *hadn't* done in the past.

He swallowed. "I'd like to take all of this data, organize it by category, run it through some business management software and figure out just where MCS is financially."

Mitzy's smile remained in place but he thought he saw it tighten a notch or two. "How long will that take?" she asked.

"It's hard to say exactly. I'm guessing a couple of hours every evening for a few weeks." Which would not only give him time to do a very thorough accounting of the last two years, but educate Mitzy on the issues before she had to make any hard decisions. He leaned back in the desk chair and met her contemplative gaze. "The question is, where would you like me to do this? Here, or at my ranch?"

She ran her finger along the edge of the desk.

Once again, it looked like they were on the same page.

"Here. Definitely," she said. A long heated look passed between them.

Happy he would have an excuse to see her as well as an

opportunity to make good on his secret promise to Gus, Chase worked another hour while Mitzy went off to hang the wreath on the front door and get caught up on a few chores while the quads slept.

He was just about to stop for the evening when Mitzy's phone rang.

Her soft melodious voice floated out to him, stopping him in his tracks. "No, no, you stay with her at the hospital. I've got this covered...Yes. Give her my best...Thanks."

Chase walked out of the study. Mitzy was standing in the kitchen, phone in hand, looking stressed and uncertain. Again, his heart went out to her. She was shouldering so much right now. Too much. "Problem?" he asked gently.

Her eyes took on a turbulent sheen. "That was the volunteer who was supposed to help me with the quads. Her mom fell and broke her hip, so she's not going to be able to make it tonight or any other for the next few months."

"Is that going to be an issue?"

Her shoulders took on a defeated slump. She confided with wry regret, "It wouldn't have been if I was still using two volunteers at a time. But I decided over the weekend to try going down to one, at least for this evening. She was my ten p.m. person."

Absorbing her worry and concern as if it were his own, he moved closer. Suddenly, it was all he could do not to pull her into his arms and kiss her. "I could stay."

She looked at him as if aware he was holding something back. And just like that the barbed wire fence went up around her heart again. She went perfectly still. "You wouldn't mind?"

For both their sakes, he adopted her brisk, matter-of-fact tone. "Not at all."

She smiled with relief, as they found themselves firmly back in the just-friends zone. "Well," she said, straightening to her full height, her expression perky, "as long as you are up for that, cowboy, maybe you could help me with something else pretty special, too."

"Their first Christmas card photo," Chase repeated, when Mitzy had finished explaining.

He had seen it on one of her to-do lists, but hadn't expected to actually be helping with it. Now that he was, he couldn't help but feel a little proud to be included in such an important endeavor.

"Yes. I need to do it when they first wake up if they're in a good mood, and…" Mitzy beamed as she led the way into the family room, where all four bassinets were lined up in a row. She clapped her hands in delight. "It looks like they are!"

Chase stood next to her, taking in the sweet and cozy familial scene. Joe was smiling and cooing. Zach was wide-eyed and content. Alex was wrestling his arms out of the swaddling. Gabe, on high alert.

Okay so far. How long that would last was anyone's guess. "Where and how are we going to do this?" he asked, ready to spring into action.

Mitzy rested her index finger against her chin. Excitement shimmered in her melodic voice. "I was thinking I could prop them up against the pillows on my bed." She shifted so quickly her shoulder brushed his.

Ignoring the resultant pressure against his fly, he kept his eyes locked with hers.

"I've already got a velvety white blanket laid out as a backdrop. All we need to do is change their diapers and put them in their little Santa suits and caps. That is—" she finally paused to take a breath, her elegant brows lifting and her teeth worrying her lower lip "—if you're game."

How could he turn her down? How could he turn *any* of them down?

Still wishing he could kiss her, he briefly let his hands rest on her slender shoulders, then said, "I am. So…" He grinned, stepping back to accept the infant she put in each arm. "Let's do it."

Together, they went up to the nursery. They worked in tandem, with Chase ridding the boys of their damp sleepers and diapers, and Mitzy coming along behind to swiftly get them dressed.

Finished, they took the babies into her bedroom. Chase laughed as he took in the mahogany sleigh-style headboard, which had been draped with the prelit garlands and decorative red velvet bows he'd brought her. "You were busy while I was working," he teased.

"Mmm-hmm." Mitzy arranged the four baby boys side by side on the center of her king-size bed. With Chase watching over them, she got her digital camera from the bureau. "Okay, my little darlings, say 'merry Christmas!'" she said.

Joe pursed his lips out and cooed. Zach stared off into space. Alex swung his arms so fast and wide he hit his brother Gabe in the face.

Gabe howled. Alex threw out his arms again, this time hitting a startled Zach who, unlike Gabe, did not verbally complain but, knocked slightly off balance, startled and sort of fell sideways.

"Oh, dear." Mitzy handed Chase the digital camera, and went in to comfort Gabe and straighten Zach.

Eventually, thanks to her amazing skills as a mommy, all was well again. "Do you want to do the honors this time and snap the pic?" she asked over her shoulder, holding a stuffed animal aloft for the infants to focus on.

"With pleasure." Chase got them all in frame and

clicked the button several times as Alex wiggled around once again, this time causing a chain reaction of falling to one side.

"How are the pictures?" Mitzy asked, beginning to sound a little worried.

Chase checked. He knew if she saw them she'd be disappointed. The boys were cute as could be, but this rendering did not accurately depict that. Not even close, in fact. "Um, they're a little blurry in that action-photo way," he said. "Nothing Christmas card ready, unfortunately."

They tried again, no more successfully.

Thinking it would be a shame to settle for a subpar photo, Chase had an idea. "Why don't you get in the picture, too?" he asked.

"I...can't." She touched her hair. "I haven't had time to do anything special..."

She didn't need anything special.

Although he knew when she sat for family photos in Dallas for Judith, it was a huge production. The ones they had done for their engagement had been even more elaborate, and though he'd went along with it for Mitzy's sake, he'd detested every moment of it.

"You look beautiful. But if you want to brush your hair again or put on some more lipstick or something, go for it. I just think they might be happier on your lap and in your arms."

Mitzy rushed into her closet, then the adjacent bath, while Chase stretched across the bed and amused the quads with his rendition of "Santa Claus Is Coming to Town." Several minutes later she came out and his breath caught in his throat. She had changed into a trim black skirt and a pretty red silk shirt. Her hair was down and newly brushed, eyes and cheeks glowing with excitement, her lips possessing a soft, sexy sheen.

His eyes met hers. "Gorgeous," he said.

She flushed in relief. "Thanks."

Together, they worked to get her situated against the pillows, all four of her babies in her arms.

"Uh-oh," Mitzy winced, when Chase got ready to take the photo.

He put down the camera. "What?"

Embarrassment gleamed in her eyes. With her arms still full of four happy babies, she said, "My skirt."

Oh, man. It had ridden halfway up one thigh. He didn't know if it would show in the photo, but clearly she didn't want to take the chance.

He cleared his throat. "Want me to see if I can fix it?"

She nodded, looking even more mortified.

Chase put the camera down and reached across the bed. Very carefully, he slid his fingers beneath the hem and ever so gently tugged.

It came down about four inches, but wasn't going to budge beyond that.

Blood rushing to his groin, he straightened. "I think that's going to be okay."

She nodded. "Thanks." Her throat sounded as clogged as his felt.

Figuring they better get to it before he got even more aroused, Chase picked up the camera and said, "Ready, boys?"

Apparently really liking where they were, all four looked up at Mitzy adoringly. Chase snapped a dozen photos. All were slightly different, with varying expressions on the boys' faces, but each and every one of the images captured the pure, abiding love flowing between Mitzy and her quadruplets. "Got it!" he said, just as the babies, beginning to tire, started to squirm.

Working as a team again, they fed the babies, burped them and then tucked them into their cribs.

It was close to midnight when they finally eased out of the nursery and headed back down the stairs to the foyer. Looking no more eager to end their evening than he was, Mitzy shook her head and said, "I don't know how to thank you for this."

The desire Chase had been suppressing all evening came roaring back. He tightened his fingers on hers and tugged her close before she could glide away. "I can think of a way…"

Suddenly, there was a way-too-alluring sparkle in her eyes. "Chase…" She leaned against the coat closet and gazed up at him.

He dropped his grip on her hand, planted a palm on the wall, just beside her head, and leaned in. "Kiss me, Mitzy," he whispered, and then bent down and did what he had been wanting to do all night. And damned if she didn't kiss him back as if this were what she wanted, too.

Mitzy hadn't kissed a man like this in forever.

In fact, she'd never kissed anyone like this but Chase. But as he moved his tall, muscular body in until he was flush against her and delved into the kiss with breathtaking precision, she began to see what she had been missing.

It had been years since she'd been wanted like this, or felt like a woman with needs.

Chase brought it all back.

The feel of her heart slamming against her ribs.

The blossoming heat that started in the middle of her chest, and spread outward over her ribs, then lower still. Into a deep throbbing awareness between her thighs, a boneless feeling in her knees.

She was light-headed with pleasure as his lips touched one corner of her mouth, then the other, then moved in again to the center, probing deep. Teasing, tempting, loving and reassuring.

Her body went soft with pleasure and she wrapped her arms about his neck. Wishing they'd never broken up.

Never spent the last ten years apart.

But they had, so…

She had to be sensible. Even if it stung.

One hand splayed across the center of his chest, she wrested her lips from his and drew back.

"This wasn't part of the arrangement," she breathed, aware her hips were still tilted into the conquering hardness of his.

He took her face in his hands, kissed her temple, then drew back, raw desire still blazing in his eyes. "Maybe not yet," he murmured in return, kissing her again, even more tenderly and persuasively this time. "But it soon will be."

Chapter Five

"Why so glum?" Chase asked early the following evening when Mitzy met him at the door. He'd have thought that she would have been walking on air all day after the heated good-night kisses they had shared. He sure had been.

She pressed her lips together. "I had another disagreement with my mother."

No surprise there. Judith was always pushing Mitzy. And Mitzy pushed right back.

He took off his coat and handed it to her. "What about?"

Mitzy hung it up for him, then turned back to face him.

Tonight, she was a lot more casually dressed, as if she hoped making less effort would erect boundaries that would keep them from getting any closer.

Not a chance, given how much he wanted her, and how breathtakingly beautiful she looked with her honey-brown hair swept up into a messy knot on the back of her head.

Bypassing the study, for now, Mitzy led the way to-kitchen island, where she had been working on laptop computer.

With a soft sigh, she lamented, "I made the mistake of sending my mother the photos we took last night, along with my selection for my Christmas postcard."

As they moved into the warm, brightly lit room, he took a moment to survey her. "And what did she think?"

Briefly, hurt tautened Mitzy's pretty features. "She didn't like any of them."

He frowned. "You're kidding." He took the padded leather stool next to hers, noting Mitzy had the offending pictures on-screen.

She rested her elbows on the quartz island top, and as he looked over at her, he could see how vulnerable the rejection had left her. Her eyes glimmered moistly and her lower lip was trembling slightly. "She thinks the ones of the boys alone are not flattering enough, and she really hates the ones of me holding them."

He wrapped an arm about her shoulders. "I love those."

Twin spots of color brightened Mitzy's high cheekbones. "She said I'm…disheveled."

He brought her around to face him, so they were now sitting knee to knee. "Like hell," he said gruffly. "You're gorgeous." Then and now!

Mitzy swallowed as if she didn't know how to handle that pronouncement—or him. "In any case," she reported glumly, looking down at the hands twisted in her lap, "Mother said she would rather die than have any of those pics sent out to her friends."

Chase took her hands in his. He was furious on her behalf. "Judith said that?"

Mitzy shrugged. "I'm paraphrasing, but the drift was the same."

Chase tightened his fingers on hers. "What does she want you to do?"

Disappointment and sadness mingled in Mitzy's gaze. With a deep, energizing breath, she lifted her chin. "Have them sit for formal Christmas portraits, individually and together, when I take them to Dallas for their official debut during Judith and Walter's annual holiday open house on December 15."

Typical. And wrong. So very wrong.

Chase watched her slide off the stool and disengage their clasped hands. "What are you going to do?"

Mitzy shrugged, still not answering, and went to the fridge. "Sorry. I haven't eaten yet." She slanted him a glance over one slender shoulder. "Have you?"

He shook his head, trying not to notice how nicely her shirt cloaked the soft curves of her breasts. "Not since lunch." Which had been late.

She bent down to rummage around the lower shelves of the fridge. "Leftover lasagna and salad okay with you?"

He turned his glance away from the denim snugly cupping her delectable derriere. "More than fine."

He made a mental note to show up with dinner the next evening. Just in case.

He cleared his throat, as she got out a couple of plates, too. "So, back to the holiday cards… You must have some thoughts about what *you* want to do."

Which in his view was all that mattered.

She put down the serving spoon and walked over to his side, inundating him with her lavender baby powder scent. "Well, initially, I was just going to send this one." She pointed to the photo of the quads in her arms, all looking adoringly up at her. "But now I'm feeling self-conscious, like maybe I will regret just slapping something together."

This was the old Mitzy, the not-quite-so-confident girl

he'd become engaged to, not the polished, self-assured woman she was now.

"What does the commonsense side of you say? You know," he teased, "the social worker side that is good at finding solutions in impossible situations?"

Mitzy went back to plating food, putting it in the microwave to heat. "To send out the one that you and I thought was great to all my friends here in Laramie. And humor Mother with the formal portrait sitting when we do go to Dallas, since she is their grandmother, after all."

"See?" Chase rose to help her bring the food and silverware over to the island. "Problem solved."

"I wish!" She minimized the photos and pulled up another split screen. This one bearing what looked to be two proposed schedules of holiday events.

She gave Chase a beleaguered look. "That was only the beginning of our little tiff." Mitzy frowned as she dressed the salad. "Mother went back to the whole 'this is their very first Christmas, and I'm never going to make it special enough for them on my own' routine. And she says we need to come to Dallas for the duration of the season because I've already gotten all these invitations and she's already planned all these great events for me and the boys."

Chase studied her. "And that's not what you want."

"No." Mitzy took a bite of lasagna. "I spent my childhood from age five on with one parent or the other. My holidays with Dad were cozy and warm and relaxed with all sorts of spur-of-the-moment holiday stuff. The highlight of which was the MCS Christmas party at the saddle shop."

Chase savored the layers of Bolognese, pasta and béchamel, too. "And your holidays with Judith…?"

Mitzy ran her fork through her food. "Were overscheduled to the max." She sat back in her stool and locked eyes with him. "I'm not saying some of it wasn't great. I loved going to see the *Messiah* performed by the choir. And *The Nutcracker.* The stage version of *The Christmas Carol...*"

Her expression turned sweetly sentimental.

"Mother took me to weekend cooking camp at this ritzy resort, where we both learned how to make every holiday dish imaginable. And every year we picked out a theme and all-new decorations for the massive tree in their formal sitting room."

Chase cleaned his plate while she forced herself to take a few more bites.

"But the boys aren't old enough for any of that. And what Mother does have planned for us, as you can see—" she turned the laptop screen toward him yet again "—is either for adults only, or...like this Intro to Art program at the museum...is something the boys are likely too young to enjoy."

"Way too young," Chase agreed.

"Which is why." Mitzy pulled up yet another screen on the computer. Her expression triumphant, she showed him two columns. One had activities planned by Judith in Dallas, the other, activities that Mitzy could enjoy with her boys here in Laramie.

He sensed a mother-daughter quarrel coming up.

"What is this? A competition?" Chase asked, only half joking.

"No." Mitzy's lower lip shot out. "It's me taking charge of my life, and my sons' lives." Her eyes shimmered. "It's me demonstrating to my mother that as much as I love her—and I *do* love her—that I've got this."

Chase fell silent. Mitzy paused, reading him with her customary skill. "You don't approve?"

He carried his plate over to the dishwasher, slid it inside. "I know Judith."

She brought her dishes over, too. "And?"

He focused on the pulse throbbing delicately in her throat. Figuring he owed it to Mitzy to be straight with her, he said, "If you show Judith this list…if you make this holiday into a competition between mother and grandmother… it will be like throwing down a gauntlet."

With a frown, she touched the clip on the back of her head, took it out and massaged her scalp. "You don't think I should go there?"

It was a loaded question. One that in the past, Chase would have sidestepped at all costs. But being indirect had cost them, too.

So, like it or not, he had to tell her what was on his mind, and then hear what was on hers. "I think you should keep in mind what is really important here," he told her gently.

Guilt flashed. "The boys."

He nodded, feeling abruptly emotional, too. "And that this is their very first Christmas," he said in a rusty-sounding voice, "and it should be, above all…"

"Harmonious." She guessed where he was going with this.

"At the very least."

Mitzy sighed, looking glummer than ever. "Good luck to me achieving that!"

"Ready to call it quits for the night?" Mitzy asked, several hours later.

Chase looked up from his own laptop computer, surprised that several hours had passed. "Next shift coming in?"

"Ah, no." Mitzy slid her hands beneath her elbows. She approached him warily. "That's what I wanted to talk to you about." Releasing a deep breath, she inquired, "Would you mind giving me a hand with the babies next changing and feeding before you leave?"

He had been hoping she would ask. "My pleasure." He stepped away from the analysis he had been doing. "Did your volunteer bail on you again?"

"No. I knew you were going to be here working on the other stuff, so I didn't schedule anyone tonight."

"Planning to draft me?"

Her smile was shy. "Do you mind?"

"I like spending time with all of you." *More than you could ever imagine*.

Together, they went into the family room, where the babies were waking up. Mitzy already had the essentials laid out. Chase mugged at the babies. They all paid attention, but to his disappointment, only Joe smiled back. Maybe one day…

Oblivious to the long-term nature of his hopes, Mitzy said, "Let's change them while they're still in their bassinets, and then I'll help you get settled…"

"For?"

"Your first lesson in 'two babies at a time' bottle feeding."

"Whoa." For the first time he could recall, he wasn't sure he was up to a challenge.

Mitzy touched his arm gently. "Not to worry, cowboy," she teased cheerfully. "I'll talk you through it."

As soon as the task was complete, Mitzy directed Chase to sit on the sofa. She secured a horseshoe-shaped nursing pillow with two indentations around his middle, then propped up Joe and Zach on his lap, facing him. "If you hold a bottle in each hand, you can feed them simultaneously."

Mitzy brought Alex and Gabe over, and sitting down right next to him, did the same for herself.

"Well, this is cozy," Chase said, smiling over at her.

They were so close, their bodies were touching from shoulder to knee.

Mitzy grinned. "Now, if only I could do all four at once…"

A brief, contented silence fell. Mitzy held the bottles at just the right angle. Chase followed her lead. The boys suckled contentedly, occasionally stopping to coo or smile.

Chase understood their happiness.

Mitzy had made a very cozy, loving home for them.

Wishing, for a wild, crazy moment, that he were the daddy instead of just a family friend, Chase looked over at her and observed softly, "You seem happier." *Prettier, too. If that was even possible…*

"Yeah," she sighed ruefully. She admitted, "I was a little grouchy earlier. Talking to you helped."

He was glad to hear that he had helped. Because he would do anything to make her happy, see her smile, to make up for all those lost years when he hadn't been there for her. And wished like hell he had been. He wanted her to be able to trust him to make her happy again.

"In any case—" Mitzy's eyes sparkled contentedly "—our conversation gave me the incentive to come up with a better plan."

Aware he couldn't wait to hear it, he paused to burp Joe then Zach. "Which is…?"

Smiling confidently, she did the same with Alex and Gabe. "I'm going to strike a bargain with Mother. The boys and I will go to Dallas for their debut on the fifteenth as requested. But my cooperation with Mother's agenda has limits. Which is where you come in."

Chase lifted a brow.

"I was hoping you'd go with me that weekend, since I'm going to need someone to drive with us." She blushed. "But if it's too much, or you have other plans," she amended hastily, "I could always ask your sister, Lulu. Or maybe Rio Vasquez to go with me."

Talk about a bad idea. Chase pointed out grimly, "Rio's got a huge unrequited crush on you."

Her spine stiff with indignation, Mitzy rose. She put the sleepy, sated babies back in their bassinets, one at a time. "How would you know?" she challenged.

Chase stood, too. *Because I've got eyes*, he thought, but said, instead, stepping closer, "Because I've got a crush on you."

She stepped back. Correcting icily, "Did. Past tense."

Do. But sensing she wasn't ready to hear that, at least not tonight, he let it go.

"And you're wrong about that." Mitzy gathered up the soiled diapers and took them to the pail in the laundry room. "Rio and I are just friends."

Chase felt a surge of red-hot jealousy. He picked up the empty baby bottles and took them into the adjacent kitchen. "Does Rio know that?"

Mitzy came toward him. "Of course."

Chase planted his hands on his waist. "You're telling me Vasquez's never put the moves on you or asked you out?"

Mitzy walked past him to the sink. "He has asked me out." She pumped soap into her hands. "*Once* a long time ago. But—" she scrubbed her palms with energy "—we talked about it and agreed we would be better off friends."

Figuring it wouldn't hurt, Chase lathered up his hands, too. "And he's never tried to hook up with you since?"

"He's never tried to hook up with me, period, cowboy." She shook off the water furiously. "Unlike *some* people here who shall remain nameless."

Beginning to realize the last thing he ever wanted from Mitzy was to be put in her "friend zone," he shut off the tap and handed her a dish towel. "If you're looking for an apology for the kisses we've laid on each other recently…"

She scoffed, "Please. I know better than that!" She calmed herself with effort. "But back to the important question." Suddenly on edge, she paused to look him in the eye. "*Are* you willing to go with me to Dallas?"

Instinct told him there was something else going on here. "To run interference between you and Judith," he affirmed.

Caught up short, Mitzy waved an airy hand. "And… discourage…a few people."

"People," Chase repeated. This was like pulling teeth.

Mitzy inhaled. "Mother's planning to introduce me to a number of wealthy suitors."

The news hit him like a punch to the gut. He didn't want her going out with anyone but him. He kept his gaze locked on hers. "You're not interested?"

She looked at him like that was the dumbest question ever. "These men are all looking to get married, Chase."

They had nothing on him. "Well, what do you know," he said, aiming a thumb at the center of his chest, "so am I."

Refusing to get the hint, Mitzy rolled her eyes. "Maybe I should let my mother fix you up, then."

"Okay," he said.

She tensed with obvious jealousy.

Satisfaction roaring through him, he qualified, "As long as it's with you."

Her lips formed a round O of surprise. "Chase Mc-Cabe." She planted her hands on her hips. Glared. "What has gotten into you this evening?"

Aware he hadn't felt this called to task since high school, he shrugged. "The Christmas spirit?"

She looked him up and down, reminding archly, "We're supposed to be seeking out closure!"

He met and held her gaze. "As long as we're putting an end to everything bad or sad that ever happened between us, I completely agree. I do want to move on." His voice caught. "More than you know, darlin'."

A pulse throbbed in her throat. "And as for the rest of it?" she inquired hopefully.

He caught her hand and squeezed. "I want to hold on to everything good and wonderful we ever shared."

She sighed wistfully. "Wouldn't that be a nice Christmas present—for both of us," she murmured.

Happy to discover he was getting to her as much as she was getting to him, he looked her affectionately up and down. "And speaking of all things Christmas..." He winked and gallantly took her by the elbow.

Her caution returned, as swiftly as it had fled. She dug in her heels. "What are you doing now?"

Smugly, he promised, "You'll see." He guided her beneath the sprig of mistletoe hanging just above the entryway between the living room and the foyer.

Mitzy looked up, stunned. Blinked. Once and then again. "How in the world did that get there?"

He wrapped both arms around her and guided her toward him, so they were touching length to length. "I'm helping you decorate."

Then doing what he had wanted to all evening, he kissed her, softly and persuasively at first, then with growing intensity, until nothing was held in check.

He had counted on her mouth to be as soft and sweet as ever. However, he hadn't expected her to immediately rise up on tiptoe, thread her hands through his hair and kiss him back passionately, as if this were what she had been waiting for all evening, too.

Chase could feel the surrender of her body in the trembling of her knees, and the tautening of her nipples as they pressed against his chest. And yet there remained a vulnerability and confusion beneath all the mixed signals she had been giving him. A sign that said it would be best to wait until she was a little more sure of her feelings before they jumped back into bed again.

Forcing himself to take the high road, he reluctantly let her go. And just that quickly, her mercurial mood changed again. "I'm sorry." She dropped her head against his shoulder.

He smoothed a hand down her spine, still savoring the feel of her soft, warm body pressed up against him.

"For what, darlin'?" He inhaled the floral scent of her shampoo and pressed a kiss into the silky mane on the top of her head. "For making out with me?"

Mitzy jerked in an unsteady breath. "That, and for the way I've been up and down emotionally all evening." She paused to look up at him, her pretty gaze more turbulent than ever. "I thought I was moody after the birth, but—" she drew another deep enervating breath "—in the last few weeks…"

Or in other words, since he had come back into her life, Chase thought.

"…I seem to be nothing but raging hormones."

As was he.

"Hey." He waggled his brows. "I like your hormones. Especially when they lead to—" he inclined his head, indicating what had just happened "—*that.*"

Delicate brows knitting together, she pushed away from him. "I'm serious, Chase. We can't just fall back into a relationship where we left off, as if nothing ever happened to break us up, because we're both alone at Christmas and it's convenient."

Convenient? Was that all it was to her?

Or was she now trying to fool herself, too?

He said nothing.

She went very still. "Are you agreeing with me?" Her nostrils flared. "Or disagreeing?"

"Depends." He lifted both palms in a casual display of surrender. "What will get me in the least amount of trouble with you right now?"

With a huff of temper and a withering glare, she marched back to the foyer, leaving him no choice but to follow.

Aware it was past time to say good-night, he reached past her to retrieve his coat from the front hall closet. His laptop computer from the study.

She was already at the front door, waiting, her hand on the knob, when he emerged from her late father's work space. Not sure whether she was more furious with him—or herself—Chase told her quietly, "You can't script this, Mitzy. Much as you might like to."

And on that note, he bid her good-night.

Chapter Six

Mitzy was still feeling guilty and upset the next morning, so she apologized to Chase via the simple text message: Sorry I was rude. Friends?

It took him a while, but he finally texted back: Friends.

For both their sakes, they didn't speak of his incredibly persuasive kisses or her emotional post-make-out outburst again, and the next two days were more of the same.

Chase arrived around eight o'clock in the evening, and spent the next couple hours in the study, working on the financial analysis. When the quadruplets woke around ten o'clock, he stopped and helped. What originally started out as being a pretty methodical changing and feeding operation gradually lengthened, until the boys were staying awake for almost two hours, interacting with each other and gazing adoringly up at her and Chase.

Still, midnight eventually came. The boys drifted off to sleep again, and Chase always gallantly took his leave. But not before managing to steal at least one kiss that practically knocked her socks off.

Friday evening, however, was different.

He looked serious as he went into the study and began packing up his things. "Same time tomorrow evening?" she said lightly, aware how easy it had been to get used to having him around.

Chase powered off his laptop and slid the stack of handwritten notes he'd been making into the briefcase, too. His lips took on a rueful curve. "Actually, I've gone about as far as I can with my analysis, with the information I have thus far. You're going to have to go to the MCS workshop and get the rest in person if you want me to be able to complete the audit and give you a much fuller picture of where things stand financially. And then of course make recommendations on what you might want to do next."

Mitzy studied him. "But you think the business is in real trouble, don't you?"

His tall frame radiating barely leashed energy, he settled on the edge of the desk, stretched his long legs out in front of him and braced a hand on either side of him. "From what I've been able to glean so far? Yes. It looks like there has been a 20 percent downturn in sales in the last year."

Which was really bad.

The corners of his sensual lips lifted in a reassuring smile. "But MCS is still in a position to be turned around if you act now. Which is why—" he paused to deliberately hold her eyes "—you have to talk to the employees and get a fuller picture of what's been going on, what the problems are—in their view."

Mitzy hesitated, wary of ruining anyone's holidays. Suddenly feeling a little cold, she reached for the cozy cardigan sweater draped over the back of the reading chair and shrugged it on. Or tried to—the ends of her hair got tangled up in the shawl collar. "I'd like to avoid that until after New Year's."

Chase stepped up to assist, his warm fingers brushing the back of her neck in the process and causing a flurry of goosebumps.

When he'd finished helping her, he settled his hands on her shoulders and guided her around to face him. "Knowing you're concerned—that you *care*—might *make* your employees' holidays."

Mitzy paused as his resolute advice sunk in. "I hadn't thought about it that way," she returned softly.

Chase grabbed his briefcase with his right hand and wrapped his left arm about her shoulders. Together, they walked toward the foyer. "I imagine everyone is feeling your father's absence, and worried about what the future holds. The craftspeople would probably welcome the chance to share their views with you."

"Okay. I'll go in Monday morning, first thing. It'll give me a chance to see how the plans are going for the annual Christmas party, scheduled for the twenty-second. And also find out how to calculate the annual bonuses, which are usually given out then."

She slowed her pace as they reached the coat closet. "In the meantime, I've got to get going on the domestic front."

His brow lifted.

Mitzy sighed her regret. "My mother was right about one thing. I haven't done enough to get in the holiday spirit." She looked around at the lone sprig of mistletoe decorating the front of the house.

There might be a wreath on her front door and garlands still decorating her king-size bed, courtesy of Chase, but... "I haven't even gotten a tree yet."

He shrugged into his coat. "Want me to help with that?"

This time it was she helping him with his collar. "You're

not too busy?" she asked, her fingers tingling as she brushed the satiny warm skin of his nape.

Chase's gaze softened with aching tenderness. He wrapped his arms about her waist and brought her close. "Haven't you figured it out yet?" he murmured, lowering his face to hers and looking deep into her eyes. "I'm never too busy for you."

Feelings rushed over her as their lips met, and it was more than just the combustible chemistry between them that was turning her world upside down. It was the way he was present in a way he never had been when they'd been previously involved. The way he'd been able to step back, when all she really wanted to do was leap forward.

And suddenly Mitzy realized they were still doing what they'd been doing for the last ten-plus years.

Wasting time.

Way too much time, as a matter of fact.

Doing what she had wanted to do all week, she tugged off his coat, encircled her arms around his neck, pressed her body against the warm hard surface of his and kissed him without restraint.

Loving the way he kissed her back.

As if there were no tomorrow, no yesterday, only right now. Here. Tonight. And maybe in the grand scope of things, Mitzy considered, dancing him backward toward the stairs, tonight was really all that did.

Chase made a low sound of pleasure in the back of his throat and smiled, while they kissed ravenously all the way up the stairs and down the upstairs hall.

She'd left on the lights that decorated the sleigh headboard of her king-size bed, and they glittered in the darkness of the room. "Festive." He grinned.

"And the perfect amount of lighting," she said.

"For?"

"Seeing only what I want you to see."

Her body had changed since they'd last made love. "I've got stretch marks, a C-section scar…"

"Don't care." He helped her get off her sweater, jeans, undies. She stripped him down, too. He threaded his hands through her hair. "You're still beautiful."

She felt beautiful, when he kissed her like that.

Womanly.

And hot. So hot…

The next thing she knew, he was stepping back, pausing to take her in. His eyes roving the fullness of her breasts, the nip of her waist, before sliding down to encompass her hips and thighs. "Really beautiful," he rasped.

Clasping her to him, he kissed her again, with startling possessiveness, bringing her closer still, enveloping her with his warm, hard strength. She shivered as his fingertips and then his mouth caressed the curves of her breasts, the taut aching tips.

Lord, she had missed this, missed *him*…

Thrilling at his touch, she drew him back to her bed. Eager to explore his body, too, to make up for lost time, she lay facing him. Still kissing, their fingertips roved. She felt the hard ridges of muscle, lower still, the throbbing velvety heat. He found her wetness, stroking, teasing, until nearly delirious with want and need, she shimmied up against him. Her pulse pounding, she pressed her lips to his, feeling wild, wanton. His breath was hot against hers, the lazy ministrations of his tongue tangling with hers, giving her a whole-body shiver.

The exploratory nature of their touching brought them closer yet. But only when she was writhing with hot, burning desire, until there was no doubt how much they needed each other, needed this, did he part her thighs and move between them. Taking this gift for what it was, she caught her breath as pleasure flooded her in hot, irresistible waves. And then there was no more holding back. He retrieved a condom. She sheathed him. He rolled her onto her back, cupped her bottom and took her slowly, sweetly.

She took him deeper, accepting the feeling of belonging that he gave her, shuddering as he demanded more. And then there was nothing but the hot mesmerizing slide of pleasure, the building heat and friction, the magic of their connection that had them soaring, flying, free. And together, once again.

Afterward, Chase felt Mitzy's usual thoughtful manner return as their shudders subsided, their breathing slowed.

Aware this was likely an impulsive action on her part— a way of taking command of the unexpected flare of unmanageable feelings between them—he drew the covers around her.

He was also aware that did not make their lovemaking any less significant. Whether she realized it or not, this had been an important first step to reconciliation. Not a step toward the closure she had once said she wanted, or a way to say goodbye to the love they had shared in the past.

Still holding her close, he pressed a kiss into the fragrant softness of her hair. "Doing okay, darlin'?" he asked gently.

She lifted her head. Put her fist on his chest, and rested her chin on that. "I want to say this was a mistake—the kind I usually caution others about."

He kept her close. "But?"

She tilted her head at him, feisty as ever. "It didn't feel like an error in judgment. It felt right."

He ran his hands through the tousled ends of her hair. "To me, too," he admitted huskily.

She bit her lip and paused.

"Then?" he prodded.

Sighing, she rolled over onto her back, and lay her forearm across her eyes. "I don't want whatever this is between us to end as badly as our relationship did before."

"It won't," Chase promised, rolling onto his side. He studied her quietly. "If we take it a step at a time."

She lifted her forearm to peer at him. "And what step would this be?" she returned wryly.

Ignoring the doubt suddenly gleaming in her eyes, he shrugged. "The first one in the right direction."

She worried her bottom lip with her teeth.

His knee touched hers beneath the sheets. "Sound about right to you?"

This was what she wanted, wasn't it? Not to rush. Or make any of the myriad mistakes they'd incurred before?

Her aquamarine eyes sparked again—with an entirely different emotion. She nodded, reaching for him again. "Sounds perfect," she murmured, as their lips met.

Mitzy and Chase made love one more time, their encounter as sexy and thrilling as ever. Before he left, he told her he'd be by the next day to help her with getting a tree—the old-fashioned way.

And sure enough, he arrived Saturday afternoon, looking like the cowboy he'd been raised as, in a flannel shirt, vest, boots and jeans.

They loaded up all four boys in her SUV.

Content to let him drive, she relaxed in the passenger seat. "So where is this perfect place?" she asked, as they headed out of town, her body still humming from their unexpected lovemaking the night before.

"My place. The Knotty Pine Ranch."

Trying not to notice how masculine and capable he looked behind the wheel, she laughed at the double entendre. When he wasn't working, he could be such a tease. "Did you really name it that?"

He slanted her an ornery glance. "Wait and see."

Fifteen minutes later, she did.

There it was, bold as ever on the black wrought iron archway that fronted the entrance to his property. She surveyed the beautiful Texas landscape that seemed to be a rugged combination of flat land and rolling hills. "How many acres?"

"Three hundred, give or take."

"How much is pasture?"

"About a hundred. The rest, as you can see, is all woods. In which," he added significantly, "is a lot of pine."

"Ah."

"Which is where we will get our trees."

"Plural?"

"I figured we'd both want one."

"True." She looked around a little more, taking it all in. She could see him being happy out here. For that matter, she could see herself and the boys doing well in a place like this.

Not that she should be going there...

She forced her attention back to the property. "The barns are nice. So is the house."

There were half a dozen very handsome horses grazing in the fields. "All yours?"

"No." His lips twisted ruefully. "They belong to a riding academy down the road. They needed space, and I had it, so we made a deal. Their staff comes in and feeds and cares and exercises my two horses, and I let some of theirs board here for free."

"Nice."

He nodded. "Works out."

He slowed her SUV as they neared and passed the

barns, which were new and neatly maintained. Her respect for all he had achieved grew. She turned back to him. "How often are you usually gone?"

His broad shoulders relaxed. "Depends. A lot of my businesses can be managed remotely, but it's also important to regularly visit each facility. You can't substitute that for getting a feel for what is going on."

Mitzy's guilt returned. She drew a deep breath. "About Monday."

"Nervous…?"

She wished he didn't look so handsome in profile, or that she didn't react so strongly to his nearness. But some things were just beyond her control. "I feel out of my league. My dad was such a larger-than-life presence. I fear I will never be able to fill the void left with his passing."

Chase understood, which gave her the courage to admit, "When I first took over, as the new CEO slash owner, the staff assured me I didn't have to be involved in the day-to-day operations. They thought they could handle everything simply by sticking to the tried-and-true, and so did I." She shook her head miserably. "But now that presumption doesn't seem to be correct."

Chase braked, and put the SUV in Park. One hand on the wheel, he turned to her. "Look, there's no question MCS has been going through a sea change with Gus gone, but that doesn't mean it can't be put on the right track." He squeezed her hand, infusing her with a warmth and tenderness not unlike his lovemaking.

He finished soberly, "It absolutely can be with the right guidance."

Which she did not have the experience or knowledge to give. Yet, anyway.

But maybe with Chase by her side…?

Mitzy swallowed. "I looked at the spreadsheets you emailed me, this morning. There's still a lot of data missing."

He gave her hand another squeeze. "Most of which you should be able to get from the people who work at MCS and/or the MCS bank records. You could also ask Buck Phillips directly."

"But?" She sensed his hesitation about that.

"You might not want to tip him off about what you're doing, before you get a fuller picture on your own, in case he is the problem."

Mitzy wasn't really surprised to find Chase wasn't sure whether to trust Buck or not. Because Buck didn't trust Chase, either. And hadn't since Chase had proposed the changes to MCS, years ago, that would have boosted profits and eliminated jobs, leaving some of their employees out of work.

"Because that might incent him to try and cover his tracks," Mitzy guessed.

Chase nodded. "Which would muddy things a lot."

Feeling caught between a rock and a hard place, Mitzy exhaled. "I can't imagine Buck deliberately running the business into the red."

"No one says he has," Chase returned gently. "Which is why you need to keep an open mind and gather data from every source available. So you will get a fuller picture of everything."

She wasn't used to leaning on anyone. But she was leaning on Chase. And liking it—which was a surprise. She looked down at their entwined fingers, then back up at him. She knew in the past he had been focused on her family business's financial bottom line, to their detriment, but her heart told her she could trust him on this, that he cared more about her feelings than any potential fiscal loss.

So she would go with that. "Would you mind making a list for me? Of the things I'll need to find out or ask about?"

Chase smiled. "Be happy to."

Reassuring herself that they would get this figured out, with Chase's help, she relaxed as he put the car back in Drive, and they traversed the circular drive in front of the handsome adobe ranch house with the red tile roof.

"So. How are we going to do this, cowboy?" Excited to finally be out there, she favored him with a perplexed look. "Cut down a tree for me and a tree for you, with all four babies in tow?"

He parked and cut the engine, confident as ever. "We'll figure it out. Meantime—" he slanted her a sly look "—want to see my house?"

"I do."

The babies were all awake, so they detached their infant seats from the bases, left the infants strapped in and carried them inside. There was an arched roof over the big central living area, with dining and kitchen on one side, fireplace and seating area on the other. Glass walls overlooked a central courtyard sandwiched between two U-shaped wings.

One, she soon discovered, held two guest suites and laundry, the other side held a luxuriously appointed master bedroom and bath, and a private study, not too dissimilar from the one her father had enjoyed.

They went back to the main area and set all four infant seats down on the floor. "So." Chase propped his hands on his waist. "What do you think?" he asked.

Her enthusiasm ran rampant. "I love it," she said sincerely, moving close enough to see his face. "It really seems to fit you."

He scored the pad of his thumb across her lips. "But does it fit you?"

She wanted to kiss him, too. More than anything.

But fearing how fast they were starting to get ahead of themselves, she stepped back. Warning softly, "Don't tease me about that."

He started to say something, then stopped at the sound of multiple vehicles in the drive.

Mitzy paused. "Expecting company?"

He gave her a "guilty as charged" look. "Ah—yes."

Mitzy had never liked being blindsided. She caught her breath. "Mind telling me who?"

He made a face. "My entire family."

Mitzy did a double take. *"What?"*

He lifted a palm, explaining languidly, "I had already invited them over to get their trees today. And, as you've already noted, we can't exactly manage four babies and select and chop down two full-size Christmas trees without assistance, so... I figured why not." He smiled at her persuasively, then continued in the husky baritone she loved, "Besides, everyone has missed you at the family potlucks."

It was all she could do not to smack her forehead with her hand. "You're having one of those, too?"

"Well," he said, shrugging again. "We gotta eat." Another pause. "It'll be fine, Mitzy."

Would it? Interacting with Chase's extended family on her own was one thing. Socializing with them as Chase's unofficial "date" at a family potluck, with her four new babies in tow, was something else entirely.

"You've been saying you wanted an old-fashioned Christmas for your boys." He wrapped a warm, comforting arm around her shoulders. "And what's the yuletide without lots of family?"

Indeed.

Mitzy had no chance to comment further.

The doorbell rang, and Chase went to answer it.

And the next thing she knew, the entire McCabe family

was swooping in, with Chase's handsome rancher father and tax-attorney mother taking the lead.

"Mitzy," Frank said, embracing her in a warm bear hug.

"It's been too long," Rachel said thickly, hugging her, too.

His law-enforcement brother, Dan, followed with his wife, Shelley, and their preschool-age triplets. "Which just goes to show," Dan teased, "when it comes to love, there's always hope for a happy ending."

Mitzy and Chase both groaned.

Lulu elbowed her brother. "Hey, I'm glad you're finally coming to your senses, too! How long has it been since the two of you said, 'We won't'? Ten years now?"

Cullen and his pregnant wife, Bridgett, and their infant son, Robby, came in with the beagle-retriever-mix Riot, who seemed to go everywhere with them. Cullen gently interjected, "I think Chase and Mitzy can do without the commentary, little sis."

"Cullen's right," Jack agreed, ushering in his own three preschool-age daughters. Jack was a surgeon and a widower. "I'm sure Chase and Mitzy can manage their own personal lives without any help from us."

And last, but not least, there was his brother Matt, a military vet. "Don't think you're getting out of any of the heavy lifting just because you showed up with your gorgeous ex and four babies," he warned.

"Wouldn't think of it," Chase drawled. He turned and winked at Mitzy. "I'm in this for the long haul."

And so it went, for the next five hours. Teasing, laughs, climbing back into pickup trucks and trooping through the woods in order to get eight perfect trees. One for Chase and each of his sibs, another for his parents, and then of course one for her.

By the time they finished with the tree cutting and the

brisket dinner, and then divvied up the leftovers as well as the cleanup chores, Mitzy felt as if she'd been put in a time machine and the last ten years without Chase had never been.

Chase turned to her as they waved goodbye to the last of his family and walked back inside his ranch house, where the quadruplets were sleeping contentedly in their infant seats.

Beaming, he pulled her close. "See, that wasn't so bad, was it?"

The primary thing Mitzy felt at that moment was renewed pressure. "Your entire family thinks we're on track to getting engaged again."

He inclined his head to one side, as at ease as she was tense. "We don't have to do that."

"We don't," Mitzy echoed drily. Wondering what in the world he was going to suggest next.

Chase sobered. "We could just get married."

Chapter Seven

Was he serious? He was so poker-faced it was hard to tell.

"Married," Mitzy repeated, still feeling a little stunned to even hear him bring it up.

"Yeah. I mean, why get engaged again? We've already done that. If we ever get to the point where we want to be together permanently, then why not just skip all the preliminary hoopla and move right on to the good stuff?"

Now he was smiling. In a way that made her feel much more relaxed. So she assumed that he was just speaking in casual hypotheticals and not necessarily making rock-solid plans for their future. Together, they picked up the quads and moved out to the SUV, where the tree was already strapped to the roof.

Early evening, the stars were already out, twinkling against the backdrop of the night sky. A chill was descending, and she shivered.

He set one of the carriers down gently and opened the

door. One by one they settled the safety seats into the base of the car seats.

Exhausted from all the activity, the quads slept on.

Mitzy climbed into the passenger seat next to Chase, still feeling a little rattled by the unexpected direction the conversation had taken. "So you're saying if you ever decided to get married that you'd skip the proposal?"

Although they weren't talking about the two of them specifically, she wasn't sure how she would feel about that.

"No." Chase turned up the heater to ensure they'd all stay nice and warm. "I'd propose. But then..." He looked at her, serious now. "If it were you and me... I'd want to get on with it."

If.

Was it even a possibility?

Hard to tell.

Mitzy drew a deep breath, feeling she had to ask. "And if it's not?" She shoved her hands in the pockets of her fleece jacket.

He leaned over to kiss her, lightly and tenderly, then drew back. Their gazes locked, held. "That's the problem, sweetheart," he said softly. "I've never wanted to marry anyone but you."

That *was* the problem, Mitzy concurred silently, since she had never wanted to marry anyone but Chase, either. But that didn't mean they were any more right for each other now than they had been years ago.

Yes, they had incredible physical chemistry.

Yes, she adored his family as much as the McCabes seemed to adore her.

And there was no question he would be able to fit in with her family, if things ever got serious again, too.

Mitzy knew her mother.

If Chase married her, or even professed to be truly serious about her again, Judith would welcome Chase with open arms.

As for the rest...

She and Chase did not share the same ambition.

She was content doing social work in a rural Texas county. He was building a multimillion-dollar leather goods empire by acquiring one small troubled company at a time and turning it around.

And now, as a friend, he was helping her attempt to do the same with MCS.

Granted, their shared goal had them spending a lot of time together. But what would happen when his job was finished? Would be still be in Laramie, dropping by every evening? Helping out with the quads? Or would he be on to the next business challenge, leaving her behind, the way he had done before...

Mitzy didn't know.

Didn't *want* to know.

Not until after MCS had been put back on the right track and the holidays were over.

So she forced herself not to think about it.

Not anymore that night.

And not the next day, either, when Chase came back over to help her string lights on the gorgeous pine in her family room. "So how are things going with your mother?" he asked.

Mitzy groaned and continued untangling the lights. The babies were sitting in their windup baby swings, swaying gently back and forth, and watching all the activity.

"Don't ask," she said, sending an affectionate glance to her children.

Chase plugged in the strand he had, smiling when it worked. "That bad?" he asked.

Mitzy worked out a particularly difficult knot. "Remember how I mentioned she was hiring a professional photographer to do formal portraits of all of us when I go into Dallas for the boys' debut on December 15?"

"Yes, I do." He looped the end over the top of the tree. Walked around. "And that's a problem because...?"

Finished, Mitzy stood. "My portrait comes with clothes, hair and makeup stylists. Which means hours to get ready before we even sit through it."

Chase watched her test her strand, which lit, too. "What about the boys?"

Mitzy plugged the end of her lights into his. "Mother has a wardrobe person and four nannies standing by for them, too."

"I'm surprised she didn't order hair and makeup for the little guys, as well."

Mitzy playfully punched his shoulder. "Ha-ha."

His hand touched hers as they continued positioning the twinkling lights. "Seriously, sounds like she's thought of everything."

"And that's the crux of the problem," Mitzy lamented, her whole body quivering at just one touch. Tamping down her ever-escalating desire, she looked up at Chase. "Mother probably has dreamed up a whole lot more to make this open house something *special*. She just hasn't told me what it all is going to be yet."

Chase touched the back of his hand to her cheek. Said gently, "It could all be a nice Christmas present for you this year—as well as a sweet remembrance years from now. Given how fast kids grow, and how very much you're going to want to hold on to all of these memories..."

Mitzy inhaled deeply. When he was right, he was right. "I know. It's just..." She paused as they came to the end of the strands.

"What?" Chase gathered her in his arms and smoothed the hair from her face.

The understanding in his blue gaze made it easy for her to go on. "I know she doesn't mean to, but Mother always make me feel like I'm not enough. That without her assistance, I'm lacking somehow. That I still don't understand what is really important in life."

Chase stroked up and down her spine, commiserating, "Money?"

Mitzy rested her forehead on the hard sinew of his chest. "On the surface, yes, it's that." Adding wryly, "Judith does love her luxury. But deep down, I think that it's more about security." She took Chase's hand and led him over to sit on the sofa next to her. "Mother's early years with Dad were brutal. He was always working to get his business off the ground. There was never enough money. And she had to cater like crazy to pay the bills. Which left her very little time for me."

Chase shifted her onto his lap. "When did that change?" He took her hand in his.

Mitzy looked down at their clasped fingers. "I asked her that once."

"And…?"

Mitzy sighed. "She said she was cleaning up after a party for a wealthy client, and she realized that had she only married the *right* man, that could be her life. And mine. And she resolved right then to get it. So she left Dad and moved me to Dallas, resumed catering—to the richest, most influential clients she could find—and began clawing her way up the social ladder."

"Hence the three marriages before Walter."

"Each wealthier than the last."

They fell silent.

Mitzy played with the buttons on Chase's shirt. "Mother

thinks it's easy to be happy if you have money. And impossible if you don't."

Chase nodded. "Whereas you want the middle ground," he guessed.

Another silence fell.

Figuring if they didn't get a move on, they'd never finish the tree, Mitzy rose again.

Chase followed her over to the boxes of ornaments.

"What do you think it takes to be happy?" he asked softly.

Mitzy hung a glittery red bulb, then picked up a gold. "Well, I guess it's what I had with my dad. The sense that he put my happiness and well-being above everything else. Including business."

Chase tensed.

Unable to read his expression, she continued, explaining, "Which of course is what I'm trying to do for the quadruplets. Let them know that no matter what they come first."

Chase nodded, obviously agreeing.

"And then, of course," Mitzy added honestly, "I think you have to have 'family' to be happy. Whether in a traditional sense of blood relatives or with a makeshift group of close friends."

Chase smiled and, noticing the swings were all slowing, went up to rewind them, one by one. "And children," he said, mugging affectionately at the quads.

Miraculously, all seemed to smile back.

"And children," Mitzy agreed, realizing all over again what a good daddy Chase was going to be someday.

Chase went back to get more ornaments. "What do you think about spouses?" He nudged her shoulder lightly, looking down at her. "Are those necessary?"

Heat spread from her chest into her face.

Realizing they were back on the subject of marriage again, Mitzy forced herself to be forthright. "I think it's nice when it all works out," she allowed as their gazes meshed and held for an inordinately long moment. "But I also know—" she took another deep breath "—from my time in the field, doing social work, that there are plenty of happy and content one-parent families out there. Happy and content single childless people, too."

"Hmm." Chase nodded thoughtfully.

It was Mitzy's turn to be curious. Just how hell-bent on getting hitched was Chase? Did he have someone particular in mind? Or was he still narrowing down the field?

"Hmm," she echoed, "meaning…?"

Chase hunkered down to hang some ornaments on the lower branches. Denim stretched across his muscular legs and butt. The same happened across the front, in the taut stretch over his fly.

"I can see that with my brother Jack," he said, oblivious to the effect he was having on her.

He reached to the right, and the same thing happened as the fabric molded to his buff upper body and arms. Reminding Mitzy what a fine body he had.

Chase frowned and continued sorrowfully, "He was married to the love of his life. When she died delivering their third daughter, he knew no one would ever take his wife's place. So he resolved to be happy and content on his own."

But was Jack truly happy? Mitzy wondered.

Her friends, nurses Bridgett and Bess Monroe, who worked with Jack at the hospital, did not really think that was so.

Chase inhaled and straightened until he towered over her. Shook his head and continued ruefully, "But for me…

and my brother Matt…and my sister, Lulu…we're all still looking for that happily-ever-after that's so far been elusive."

"Romantic love," she guessed, aware that she sometimes secretly felt the same. When she let herself, that was. Which, to be honest, had not been often, even before she and Chase broke up. Maybe it was her mother's many marriages, or her father's loneliness after their divorce. Or even the way Chase and the other McCabes seemed to take it for granted that they would fall in love, and marry and live happily ever after one day. All she knew for certain was that she found it nearly impossible to trust the same could or would happen for her. Even if it was what she privately yearned for, deep inside.

"And marriage, kids, pets. Basically, the whole enchilada," Chase said. He paused as if replaying what he had just said in his head. "Now who sounds like a girl."

She laughed at his self-effacing expression. "Well, whatever you call it, Chase," she said, wreathing her arms about his neck and tilting her face up to his, "you're a good guy and I hope you find that romantic love and satisfying family life that you want."

He kissed her back, softly, lingeringly. For a moment looked deep into her eyes. Contemplating tenderly. "You, too…"

The rest of Sunday was spent taking care of the quads, decorating the rest of the interior of her home, and addressing and mailing the Christmas photo postcards she had decided to send to her friends. Chase was there to assist, every step of the way, and once the babies were put down for the night, he took her to bed for a passionate round of lovemaking.

Before he left, he went over the inquiries she needed to

make at MCS the following morning, patiently explaining all the accounting terms she was unfamiliar with.

"How can you not look tired?" she asked as she walked him to the door.

He pulled her in for a lingering good-night kiss. "Don't know." He chuckled. "But you've got a big day tomorrow, sweetheart, so you better get some shut-eye."

He was right. She *was* tired. Worse, she was confused about the increasingly romantic turn in their relationship. The way they were still both holding back. She knew to jump in headfirst to a reconciliation would be foolish. Even if feminine instinct told her that was exactly where they were heading. Their first breakup had been devastating. She couldn't go through that again, any more than she could seem to turn away from him. When he was with her, she felt comforted, secure, happy. Really hopeful about the future. When they were apart, doubts crept in. The constant ups and downs left her feeling unsettled. And once again, sleep was elusive. By morning, as she headed for MCS, she was on edge.

Her conversations with individual employees, and then department heads, left her feeling even more frazzled. "I don't know why you didn't come to me when there were so many problems," she said to the group of very senior employees gathered in her office at day's end.

Sue Miller said, "We all agreed there was enough on your plate, with your dad's illness and passing, the difficult pregnancy and four infants to deal with."

"Besides, you're here now," Chet Brown added.

And Buck Phillips, who was off visiting one of their suppliers, wasn't, Mitzy thought. Although the company COO was expected in before closing.

"Yes." Pushing the guilt over her lapses aside, Mitzy smiled and said, "I am. And one of my first orders of business, in addition to tending to the various issues you-all have pointed out, is to make sure we have a really nice MCS Christmas party this year. Which should fall on Saturday, December 22, if we follow tradition. So, how do you want to do this?"

The room fell silent. Mitzy noted the definite lack of enthusiasm. Which was strange. The end-of-year holiday get-together had always been one of her favorite gatherings. Everyone else's, too. "Should I send out an email blast, or just put up a sheet in the break room, so everyone can let us know what dishes they intend to provide? So we don't end up with all potato salad or something."

Another awkward pause.

"Does this mean we can bring guests again?" Lisa Franklin asked.

Mitzy nodded. "Just let us know how many."

Yet another short silence fell. Looks were exchanged. Finally, Bart Higgins blurted out, "Are we going to get annual bonuses?"

What a strange question to ask! "Of course," Mitzy said, taken aback. "You always do."

Everyone stared at her like she had grown two heads. "Not last year," Randy O'Quinn muttered from the back.

He wasn't joking.

Nor was anyone else.

"You absolutely will have bonuses this year," Mitzy promised, embarrassed to discover the inexcusable lapse. And she would personally make sure they were more generous than ever.

The meeting concluded, just as chief operating officer Buck Phillips returned from his outside appointment. He caught her on her way out and asked to speak with her privately, a request to which she readily agreed. "What's going on here?" he demanded as she shut the door to her office behind them.

"I could ask you the same question," she said to the man who had once been her dad's best friend and most trusted coworker. "Why did you give the orders to downgrade all our materials?"

Buck stiffened. "Because it was the only way to make ends meet."

Mitzy sat down behind the desk. "Is that why there were no bonuses last year?"

Buck remained defensive. "The employees understood we did not have the funds." He squinted. "What's gotten into you, Mitzy? Is Chase McCabe behind all this? Is he the one that's got you asking for bank statements?"

So it wasn't an accident—Buck was hiding things from her, and who knew who else! Glad Chase had prepared her for just this, she returned calmly, "We need those financial records for end-of-year profit and loss statements and balance sheets."

Buck scoffed. "Your dad never needed any of that!"

Mitzy glared right back. "My dad never had trouble paying out bonuses, either."

Silence fell.

Buck's ruddy skin reddened. "I've done a good job here, Mitzy." His voice caught. Angrily, he pushed on, "It's not easy filling the void Gus left."

Mitzy shared his grief. She swallowed around the ache in her throat. "I know that."

Buck threw up his hands. "So what are you doing spending every evening talking to Chase McCabe? Is he promising to help you? Because I'll tell you what he wants," Buck stormed. "What he always wanted. Your dad's company!"

That wasn't true, Mitzy thought.

It couldn't be.

Chase hadn't once offered to buy it from her, even when her mother had suggested he do so, back at Thanksgiving.

Buck shook his head at her, as if he couldn't believe her naïveté. "I know you were in love with him once, but you can't trust him, honey, not when you and the company are both this vulnerable."

Mitzy thought about all Chase had done for her the past few weeks. How honest they had been with each other.

"Yes. I can," Mitzy asserted fiercely. But even as she spoke, she remembered the depth of Chase's ambition and felt the little niggling of doubt. And doubt—about his values, and his intentions—was exactly what had destroyed them before.

Chapter Eight

Two hours later, Chase arrived to find Mitzy on the phone. Her honey-brown hair loose and flowing, cheeks pink with agitation, she waved him across the threshold of her bungalow. "There's no need to send nannies for the trip, Mother. Chase has agreed to drive to Dallas with us…Saturday morning…Yes. Listen, we're on our way to an event. Love you, too. Bye." Finished, she cut the connection.

"Hey." She went up on tiptoe to give him a brief hug. On the way down, paused to admire his sport coat and tie. "You look nice."

His gaze drifted over her, taking in her figure-hugging pine-green sheath dress, black tights and favorite suede flats. "So do you, sweetheart."

Like they were going on a real date.

Albeit a very well-chaperoned one.

Mitzy rushed to the coat closet and brought out a co-ordinating glen plaid scarf and knee-length black winter coat. She handed him the coat, while she doubled the strip of cashmere, drew the ends through the knot and looped it around her throat. Then she dashed to the hall mirror to make sure the neckwear was centered properly.

She caught his eyes in the mirror. "I can't believe I forgot the first annual Choral Extravaganza was this evening!"

It had been on her big list of proposed yuletide activities. Smiling, he held out her coat for her. Waiting as she slipped her arms through. "I wasn't going to let you forget."

She turned to him, mischief sparkling in her eyes. "Actually, cowboy," she murmured playfully in a low, hushed tone, "you don't let me forget a lot of things."

Like what a good time they could still have together, with and without her four boys, and how much they enjoyed making love.

"Here they are, all ready to go!" Two volunteer helpers wheeled the four infants into the foyer. The boys were strapped into a quad stroller that featured two adjustable reclining seats in front, and two in a row behind them that sat slightly higher.

Chase's heart expanded at the winsome sight. "Hey, little guys." Chase knelt down to greet them. Clad in red velvet fleece outerwear, knit Santa hats, with white blankets tucked around their waists, they were beyond adorable. Joe cooed. Zach smiled. Alexander banged a fist against the stroller tray. And Gabe regarded Chase as if he had come to expect seeing him in his life.

A sentiment that went both ways.

Mitzy regarded him happily. "I figured it would be easier if we walked there."

"I agree." Chase nodded at the ladies.

Lockhart Foundation receptionist Darcy Dunlop promised, "We'll tidy up before we leave."

"Are you going to need us later?" local Realtor Marcy Lyon asked.

"Thanks." Mitzy held the front door while Chase pushed the stroller across the threshold. "Chase and I've got it."

Together, they lifted the stroller down the four steps to the sidewalk and set off, companionably enjoying the winter evening. Every house had a wreath or lights strung across the porch or both. Some had yuletide lawn displays. A half-moon and a sprinkling of stars shone in the velvety black sky above. The brisk winter air was scented with wood smoke.

The boys were entranced by it all.

And Chase was captivated by the woman strolling along beside him. He'd expected her to be distraught after her visit to MCS that day, but she hadn't even brought the matter up.

He couldn't help wondering why.

"So how did it go today at the saddle company?" he asked.

Mitzy fiddled with her scarf as she stepped to the side of the stroller and let him continue to push. "I learned a lot." Briefly, she focused her attention on a yard display of Santa and his sleigh, then shifted her gaze straight ahead again. In a matter-of-fact voice she told him about the various comments she had received.

She shook her head, finally looking as stressed as he had expected her to be. "The worst thing is that I had no idea that no bonuses had been paid last year." She pressed her lips together then straightened her spine with calm deliberation. "I feel really bad about it, but I'm hoping to make it up to all the workers this year, once we figure out what our profit margin is and what we can afford. Which," she added hopefully, "should happen by the beginning of next week."

Wondering how she was going to react if his instincts were right and there was no extra money to be had in the budget this year, Chase asked casually, "Did you get all the bank statements?"

Once again, Mitzy kept her physical distance and avoided looking at him directly. "The CPA firm that's helped us out in the past is going to pick them up from the bank and prepare the balance sheet and profit and loss statements for us. That's why I'm running so late. I had to go over there and talk to them before I went home."

Chase paused as her words sunk in.

Initially, Mitzy had said she wanted *him* to do that for her. What had happened to change that? Had she somehow learned about the promise he had made to Gus? Found some other reason to mistrust him? Other than what had happened in the past?

With a sudden smile, Mitzy cocked her ear. "Do you hear that?" she said as the faint strains of "O Come, All Ye Faithful" wafted toward them. "Isn't it incredible?"

It was. She picked up her steps. Figuring talk about business could wait, he kept pace. A block and a half later, they reached the park.

It seemed like most of the town had turned out and a good deal of the rural county, as well. It was easy to see why. Every school and church choir in the area was represented. Gathered around the huge Christmas tree in the center of Town Square Park, from the smallest child to the most senior adult, their voices raised in perfect harmony.

Tearing up at the sheer magic of the moment, Mitzy knelt down to face her four baby boys. "Hear that, fellas?" she said. "That's the sound of Christmas in our hometown!"

"How about a picture to remember it by?" Chase got out his phone. He snapped several of the five of them.

Lulu walked up to join them, ebullient as ever. "How about a picture of all of you?"

Chase looked at Mitzy. To his disappointment, saw the briefest hesitation before she nodded and flashed a consenting smile. "Absolutely! Thanks, Lulu!"

Chase and Mitzy knelt and took up stations on either side of the quad stroller and moved in close. Lulu snapped several photos on his phone. Then a few more on Mitzy's cell, too.

As they scanned the results, Chase had a glimpse of what it would be like if he and Mitzy and her boys were officially a family. He'd seen so much of them lately. They'd become such a huge part of his life. He wanted that to continue, more with each passing day. He sensed, if Mitzy would let her guard down completely, she'd want more than just his business advice and help with her babies, and friendship and occasional sex, too.

"Looks good," Mitzy said, content.

Now, Chase thought, if only Mitzy would tell him what had happened to create this new tension between them, they could continue making inroads to a reconciliation. And then maybe move on to the future they always should have had.

Mitzy knew she was being a little standoffish, to say the least. She couldn't help it, now that business had come up again, in a divisive way she hadn't expected.

Worse, Chase seemed to intuit she was holding a fair amount back from him. And that wedged even more emotional distance between them.

With a sigh of frustration, Mitzy rose. She swung toward him, her body nudging his in the process. He studied the conflicted look on her face.

As much a Texas gentleman as ever, he inclined his head

at the food stands set up at the perimeter. "Want some hot cocoa?" he offered, his low masculine voice sending a new thrill through her. "Peppermint ice cream?"

Determined to keep him at arm's length, until she could figure out how to handle this new glitch between them, she backed up as much as she could without bumping into another concertgoer, which turned out to be about half a step. "How about both?" she asked, pretending she couldn't feel the sizzle of awareness between them. "I think I forgot to have dinner, I was so busy getting ready to go tonight."

His chuckle was warm and seductive. He turned to his sister. "Anything?"

Lulu shook her head. "No. I'm good."

Looking more enamored of her than ever, Chase turned back to Mitzy and touched her shoulder protectively. "Stay right here." Uncaring of the many witnesses around them, Chase brushed his lips across Mitzy's temple and gave her elbow a little squeeze. "I'll be right back."

With a restive sigh, Mitzy watched him go. His tall handsome body disappearing in the crowd.

Chase's sister slanted her a knowing glance. "You know he's never gotten over you, don't you?" Lulu said.

I've never gotten over him, either, Mitzy thought.

Which made the disloyal feelings Buck Phillips had sparked within her today even worse. The part of Mitzy that had fallen hopelessly in love with Chase, and been planning a future with him, knew he would never hurt her. However, the part of her that had broken up with him knew, when it came to business, that he still might.

Lulu gave Mitzy an empathetic look. "I really hope you two give each other another chance."

The wildly romantic side of Mitzy hoped so, too.

But the realist in her…coupled with the remembered pain of a turbulent childhood, and the experience of having vastly different divorced parents…left her unsure of what to hope for.

What should take precedence in her life? she wondered.

Finding a loving husband for herself and a daddy for her four boys?

Or should she forget all that for now and concentrate on fulfilling the promise she had made to her late father regarding his legacy?

The truth was, she wanted to do both. Simultaneously. But what if that wasn't possible? What if, she mused uncomfortably, she had to choose?

Mitzy had no answers, and she was still feeling conflicted when Chase returned, an incredible-smelling smoked turkey barbecue sandwich in one hand, a tray bearing the aforementioned peppermint ice cream and two cups of hot cocoa in the other.

"Looks like I wasn't the only one who was hungry," she noted wryly, wishing she'd thought to ask him for something healthier and more substantial, too.

As usual, he was one step ahead of her. He flashed a sexy grin. "I'm only drinking the hot chocolate. The rest, sweetheart, is for you."

Mitzy's stomach growled hungrily in response.

Chase chuckled appreciatively.

Lulu, who'd been focused on the beautiful music, rolled her eyes. "Okay, I'm going to leave you two lovebirds alone. Call me on my cell if you need anything." She disappeared through the crowd.

Chase leaned down to whisper in Mitzy's ear. "Want to find a quieter spot?"

Mitzy noted her babies were getting sleepy.

"Yes," she said, grateful as ever for Chase's thoughtfulness. "I'd like that."

With the music still soaring in the background, infusing everyone with the Christmas spirit, they made their way through the crowds to the edge of the park and found a bench. By the time they actually sat down, the quads were dozing.

As Mitzy looked over at Chase's handsome profile, guilt swept through her.

She couldn't help but feel wrong for doubting him.

Or going behind his back to get the rest of the business financials done in a way that didn't involve him. When he'd already put so much of the information together for her.

But because Buck Phillips had persisted that an outside firm was the only way to go, if she really wanted to trust the final numbers, she had relented.

And caused a tiny rift, or maybe even downright insulted, Chase in the process.

She struggled against the dawning realization that she might not be cut out to handle the complex requirements of running a business and simultaneously having a satisfying personal life. She tried to concentrate on the meal he'd brought her instead. "You didn't have to do all this," Mitzy said with an easy smile, though she was so hungry she was incredibly grateful he had.

"Yeah, I do," Chase retorted, letting out a low laugh. "You're my woman." He wrapped a strong arm around her shoulders, squeezed them briefly, then let her go so she could tend to her meal unencumbered. "And that's what a man does for his woman," he told her cheerfully. "He takes care of her."

"Okay, well, then," Mitzy drawled back, mimicking his casually affectionate tone. Trying to demonstrate how unaffected she was, she broke her luscious sandwich in two. "Now we're going to have to split this sandwich," she declared saucily, "because if I'm your woman, you're my man and—" her voice clogged unexpectedly at the memory of all they had once had and lost "—a woman takes care of her man."

Tears stung her eyes.

What was it, she wondered, about the holidays that made her so overly emotional? So prone to acting on impulse? Letting down her guard and doing really, really crazy things like making love to him, picking up where they had left off and acting like they had never spent the last decade apart?

She was a veteran social worker, dammit. She knew from experience how badly these things usually ended.

"Hey." Chase took her chin in his hand, his concern for her evident. A staggeringly uncomfortable silence fell. "I didn't mean to upset you."

Mitzy put the sandwich down. Wiped her hands on a napkin and then blotted the moisture on her face with a Kleenex she fished from her pocket. "These are happy tears, Chase."

And confused ones, too.

His eyes were dark and unwavering on hers.

"And maybe a little bit of a sugar low," she fibbed, "from inadvertently going so long between meals."

Which was also unusual. She generally took a lot better care of herself.

Rubbing his thumb across her lower lip, he regarded her with a mixture of skepticism and sympathy.

"Really." She felt compelled to insist.

He tracked the warmth seeping into her cheeks. "Then eat," he said gruffly.

Again, Mitzy offered him half.

He refused. Which was good because once she started, she was so ravenous she could not stop. Five minutes later, she had downed the whole sandwich and the ice cream, too, while he looked on approvingly.

Appreciating his protectiveness, even if she didn't need it, she dabbed the corners of her lips. "Well, that wasn't very ladylike of me," she admitted self-consciously.

He grinned and palmed his chest. "Hey. I like a woman with a healthy appetite."

The warmth within her intensified, only now it was a different kind of heat and tension. The kind that usually preceded their lovemaking. She shot him a droll look. "You always have to bring it back around to sex."

He tugged playfully on a lock of her hair and grinned again as if liking what he saw. "I didn't mention romance," he claimed with way too much innocence. But a wave of heat flooded through her as his knee bumped up against her thigh, and he waggled his brows, as if he were thinking about putting the moves on her again.

"We were talking about food," he said.

She studied him from beneath her lashes. "Sex and romance aren't the same thing."

Much as I might sometimes wish.

Although "just sex" with Chase was pretty darn amazing, too.

He met her gaze, clear now. "True."

They got up, dispensed with the trash and began strolling the quads, who were starting to be a little restless, around the perimeter of the park.

"For most people," Chase delineated further. "But," he said huskily, tucking his hands in hers, drawing her close and bending his head, "in our case, they are."

Their kiss was a melding of heat and need, love and tenderness. His lips were cold, in contrast to the heat of his tongue. He tasted like the hot chocolate they had been drinking, and Mitzy felt herself surge to life.

So what if their lives were way too complicated now? There was nothing but pleasure in this.

Nothing but the gift of finding each other again after all this time. Nothing but the hope of second chances…

Yearning spiraled through her.

Along with the sharper sense of frustration that they were in a public place.

Mitzy tore her lips from his, and still holding his face in her hands, whispered, "What am I going to do with you, cowboy?"

His eyes glowing a sensual, determined light, he leaned down and kissed her again, even more thoroughly this time.

"Just give me a chance," he said gruffly when they came up for air. She breathed in the masculine fragrance unique to him. "That's all I ask, Mitzy. Give me a chance to make everything right."

To Chase's satisfaction, the shared kisses did a lot to set things right between them once again, and the music and decorations were so festive they ended up staying another hour. By the time they walked home at ten, the babies were waking.

Mitzy warmed the bottles while Chase changed the diapers. They sat side by side on the sofa, propping the babies up on the nursing pillows, feeding then burping them two at a time.

By the time the boys were ready to be put down for the night, Mitzy looked ready to collapse. "How about I get them all settled in their cribs while you get ready for bed?" Chase offered.

Mitzy hesitated in the doorway of the nursery, appearing to think she would be neglecting her maternal duty if she handed the chore over to solely him. Chase knew she usually stayed with them, soothing and giving out pacifiers, if need be, but tonight was an exception.

"I promise, I'll come and get you right away if there are any problems."

Mitzy stifled a yawn. "Okay. I'm too beat to argue with you." With one last poignant look at Chase and her boys, she headed off in the direction of her bedroom. The upstairs grew quiet. One by one, the babies drifted off to sleep. Chase made sure the monitor was on, then walked soundlessly down the hall. A glance inside the master bedroom showed why Mitzy hadn't come back.

She was half seated on the edge of the bed, breathing deeply, eyes shut, her chin drooping toward her chest. She had a pair of pajamas clutched loosely in one hand, a black suede flat in the other.

Apparently, this was as far as she had gotten.

Chase moved closer. "Mitzy." He touched her shoulder gently. "Sweetheart."

She uttered a soft sigh. The shoe fell from her hand. Her pajamas landed on her lap. If she was this tired, Chase decided, she didn't need to wake up.

His heart swelling with tenderness, Chase guided her back against the pillows. Took the blanket draped across the end of her bed and covered her. She remained fast asleep. Determined she would get the rest she needed, he leaned down to kiss her temple, turned off the monitor, then eased out of the room as quietly as he had come in.

Mitzy woke in a state of confusion, not sure where she was or what time it was. It seemed like morning, given the daylight peeking through the blinds. But it couldn't be morning, could it? Not when she still had the 4:00 a.m. feeding to do…!

She turned to the monitor. The light indicated it was turned off. And she was…fully dressed? In the clothes she'd worn the night before…?

What the heck was going on? she wondered as she stumbled out of bed and made her way to the door. She yanked at the knob, then stumbled backward at what she saw on the other side of the portal.

Chase. Coming toward her. Dressed in the clothes he'd worn the night before, too. Sans tie and sport coat, of course. He had a day's worth of stubble on his handsome face. Crinkles of fatigue around his beautiful gray-blue eyes. "Hey—" he flashed her a grin as wide as Texas "—I thought I heard something up here. That you might be up."

Mitzy shoved both hands through her hair. "What time is it?"

Another smile. Reassuring this time. "Noon."

She took a moment to absorb that. *"Noon?"* And how could he possibly look so darn sexy? When he obviously hadn't showered, either.

"Yeah." Chase rubbed his hand over his handsomely stubbled jaw. He squinted at her happily. "You slept about thirteen hours. I was hoping you'd go a little more."

Heavens. Mitzy couldn't say when the last time that had happened. A couple of years, easy. "And the boys?" She found herself still a little off-kilter, swaying slightly.

He curved a hand around her shoulder, stabilizing her. "Are all fine." He thrust his chest out proudly. "I did their four a.m. feeding all by myself! And," he added, with mounting paternal pride, "the boys and I managed to not wake you up."

This was either the Christmas miracle she'd never expected, or some wonderful dream. Mitzy splayed both hands across his pecs. He sure felt real and warm and deliciously masculine. She swallowed around the sudden dryness of her throat. "Where did you sleep?"

Another proud moment. "On the floor of the nursery."

Deciding she really needed to use her toothbrush, she headed for the bathroom. "On the floor?"

Chase shrugged. She brushed, rinsed, spit. "Well... I wanted to be nearby in case they needed anything."

She dabbed her mouth with an ivory hand towel. "I don't know what to say."

He grinned, looking as happy as she had ever seen him. "Thank you? And maybe—" he winked sexily "—if I could borrow a toothbrush..."

She got him a spare from the drawer. Watched as he went to work. Trying not to think how intimate this all was.

Or if they were now at the point where she should give him a drawer of his own to use while he was here, or space in her closet...

Not that she had to decide today. He was here. He was happy. She was here. She was happy. It was enough.

"Seriously," she said when he had finished brushing. "This was above and beyond the call of duty."

Once again, he looked as if he wanted to kiss her.

They both knew if he did, they might not stop. "It was my pleasure, sweetheart."

Voices floated up from downstairs. Brought swiftly back to reality, Mitzy guessed, "Volunteers?"

"Yes." He walked out of the bathroom, past her bed, to the neutral territory of the upstairs hall. "Emmaline Clark, and her mother, Hedda, came at seven thirty, right on schedule," he said, taking up a station against the wall.

Mitzy settled opposite him.

"They said I could leave. They'd handle everything. But..." His glance roved her face possessively. "I kind of wanted to stay until you woke up. In case," he said with a slow, sexy smile, "you had any questions about what did or did not happen last night."

Mitzy searched her memory and came up with exactly

nothing after saying good-night to him in the nursery. Ignoring the leap of her pulse, she asked softly, "Ah. What did happen exactly?" Surely, she would remember if they had made love!

"You fell asleep sitting upright on the bed."

He wasn't joking. She buried her face in her hands and groaned. "Now I'm *really* mortified."

He leaned over to rasp in her ear, "You were cute. And tired."

Figuring it was better to see him than not be able to keep an eye on him, Mitzy dropped her hands. "Well, in any case, I owe you one."

He straightened. "Great." He lifted both arms in victory. "I accept."

Flummoxed, she said, "Accept what?"

One half of his mouth quirked up in a smile. "Your agreement to go on an actual grown-up, no-holds-barred date with me."

Chapter Nine

"Well, that was a blast from the past," Mitzy said on Wednesday, as they left the San Angelo dance hall, where they had spent a lot of time, years ago. Only this time, instead of going in the evening, they had gone in the middle of the day.

The place had been empty except for the two of them and the college kid working the lights and sound system. The music, definitely hits from a decade before. Including some of her very favorites.

"Feeling sentimental?"

Mitzy nodded. Ridiculously so. She'd forgotten what it was to look at the world with such unvarnished appreciation. To feel like everything and anything was possible. Maybe it was time she remembered.

"Good." Looking as content and hopeful as she was beginning to feel, Chase reached over and squeezed her hand. "Wait till you see our next destination."

The taco stand on the edge of the town. It looked very rough around the edges, but had some of the best Mexican street food in the area. He ordered all their favorites to go, just the way they had when they'd been dating, set them in a thermal container to stay warm, then drove back to his place. Inside the house, a picnic area had been set up, complete with pillows and blankets on the center of the floor. The flavored waters and electrolyte drinks they still guzzled in the summer heat were there, too, set in a party bucket filled with ice.

Only it was December now.

Christmas.

But the decor, which included harvest-colored disposable plates and napkins, looked like late summer, early fall. None of which actually jived with the Christmas tree they'd put up the weekend before, with the help of his entire family.

She stood, hands on her hips, gazing around. "Okay. You're going to have to tell me where you're going with all this."

He went over to turn on the lights. The tree lit up beautifully. He came back to her, lifted her hand to his mouth and kissed the inside of her wrist before offering a rakish smile. "I know what we should give each other for Christmas."

They were exchanging presents? Mitzy thought, her skin tingling at the brief intimate contact. Boy, was he leaping ahead!

Trying not to consider how easy it would be to fall in love with him all over again and want more than either was currently prepared to give, Mitzy drew an unsteady breath. "You do?" she asked hoarsely.

He wrapped his arms about her waist and brought her close so their hips and thighs were touching. "A do-over."

He stroked a hand down her spine. "I want to replace that horrible last date we had."

Mitzy's knees were suddenly wobbling. "The one where we broke up."

He aimed a heart-stopping, sexy look her way. "With a move forward instead."

She splayed her hands over the hardness of his chest, wedging distance between them. Much as they might want it to be, life wasn't magic. Or run by wishful thinking, no matter how poignant, or fantasy filled. "We can't go back."

He guided her down to the blanket to sit beside him. "But we can erase some of our mistakes. Breaking up with you, letting you break up with me, was the worst error of my life. It completely derailed me."

Mitzy tugged off her boots and sat cross-legged. "You seem to have done pretty well for yourself."

Chase shrugged, doing the same. "Professionally perhaps. And in that regard, so have you. But in here," he said, laying her hand over his heart, "all forward motion stalled." His voice caught. "In here, I'm still the same guy who fell in love with the prettiest girl in town." His smile turned tender, his glance direct. Chuckling, he asked, "Why else do you think I had my mom and dad buying new saddles every time I could talk them into it?"

Her heart did a little flip in her chest. "Because Gus and crew made the best custom saddles in the state?"

He unpacked their feast of grilled chicken and steak tacos. "Because it meant—if it happened when you were in town, visiting Gus—you'd be there at MCS." He opened up the containers of *pico de gallo*, guacamole and sour cream. "Plus, getting to know your dad paved the way for me getting a summer job at his shop, interning there during college, landing my very first job with him after."

Struggling to get her equilibrium back, Mitzy cleared

her throat, sat back and asked a great deal less sentimentally, "You did all of that to be close to me?"

"Yeah, well." He shrugged and continued as they began to eat, "I was all lusty hormones back then. And you were the girl I wanted. The *only* girl I ever wanted."

The warmth was back, spiraling up inside her. "Oh, Chase, you were the only guy I ever wanted, too."

He leaned over to kiss her.

She clung to him. "It broke my heart when we split up."

He held her close. "Mine, too." He threaded his fingers through her hair. And kissed her again, even more tenderly this time. "Which is why I want to completely erase that mistake." He put their food aside, took her by the hand and helped her to her feet. "And what better way to do it," he said, sliding a strong arm beneath her knees and swinging her up into his arms, "than by making love again, here and now."

Mitzy let out a little gasp of surprise. She had known they would end up making love again, she had even expected it to be this afternoon, but what she hadn't counted on was the way it would feel to be in Chase's home, in his bed.

He'd said she was his woman.

She felt like it as he undressed her with extraordinarily intimate pleasure. He was so strong and virile and willing to let her take them anywhere she wanted, and what she wanted was to take their time, exploring and basking in one another in the soft afternoon light.

His chest was sleek and powerfully muscled with a crisp mat of brown hair that spread across his pecs, before arrowing downward to his navel and the most masculine part of him.

As he kissed her, her fingers followed the path. Eliciting a few groans from him, and a bigger thrill for her as she found the hot, hard length of him.

Caught up in something too primal to fight, she explored him with both hands, slid between his thighs and then bent to kiss the hot, velvety maleness of him.

He groaned again, on the verge of losing control. "My turn," he rasped long moments later, turning the tables and flipping her onto her back. The next thing she knew his hands were spreading her thighs wide. He was slipping between them. Loving and caressing, until sensation spiraled through her unlike anything she had ever known. And although she had promised herself she would wait for him this time, he found a way to touch and kiss her that made her feel wanted and protected, loved and treasured, a way that sent her teetering toward the edge, and then tumbling over it.

She shuddered, her whole body throbbing, and he held her in his arms until the aftershocks passed. And still it wasn't enough. She wanted to open the packet and roll on the condom, drape herself over him as his body took on an insistent throb all of its own.

Her palms slid over his hips and she lifted him to her. Their lips fused as surely as their bodies. Lost in the pleasure, she pressed her breasts against his chest and gripped his shoulders, hard. He moved within her, trembling with a need they could no longer contain, rocking together toward the outer limits of their control.

She was part of him, he was part of her and then there was no more holding back, no more pretending that something important between them did not exist.

Mitzy didn't know if it was love or passion. Sheer excitement or a salve to loneliness. All she knew was that she needed him, and he seemed to need her, too. And it was that sweet yearning that had them connecting as never before, savoring everything about this moment, then free-floating over the edge, into ecstasy.

* * *

Unfortunately, they had a time limit because they were relying on volunteer baby wranglers, so Chase couldn't make love with Mitzy again. Not at that moment in his bed, anyway, so reluctantly, once the after shudders had passed, they'd had to get up and get dressed.

To his chagrin, Mitzy seemed as conflicted and disappointed as he was about that.

Which just went to show the sooner they could move their relationship into a more permanent arrangement—one that had all six of them under the same roof—the better.

Then he'd be able to help Mitzy, comfort and make love to her whenever, however, she needed.

But for now, it was still just a few stolen hours here and there...

Mitzy pulled on her Christmas-themed boot socks, then stood and zipped up her jeans. She gave him a wry look from beneath her lashes, then deadpanned, "For the record, I don't think it is possible, either."

Instinct told him that once again they were not on the same page.

"What isn't possible?"

She tugged her sweater over her head and spread her hands wide. "For us to simply pick up where we left off."

She was serious.

He tugged on his own boots and closed the distance between them. Irked to find them going through the cycle of passion and regret again, just because they'd acknowledged their ever-escalating feelings for each other and made love, he looked her in the eye and challenged mildly, "You don't think it can happen?"

She looked at him as if he had grown two heads. "No."

"Hate to break it to you," he rasped. He took one of her

hands and put it over his heart. Then situated one of his palms over hers. "In here?" He let his gaze drop to the regions of both their hearts. "Sweetheart, we can pretend all we like…but the caring about each other…the wanting and needing each other…it's clear now it never stopped." He paused to let his words sink in. "For either of us."

She blinked in amazement. "Which means what exactly?"

He still wanted to move at her speed, because that gave them the best chance at success. "You tell me," he rasped, albeit a little impatiently.

Once again, she intuited exactly where he was headed, and wasn't ready to go there.

She jerked free and spun away from him. "I know it would make things simpler, Chase, at least in some respects, but I can't just start wearing your engagement ring again." She stormed from the bedroom.

Personally, he didn't see why not, but aware pushing her would get them nowhere, he focused on all she hadn't said, then paused to repack their barely touched meal. "You still have it?" He had hoped that would be the case after she had tried to give the diamond back to him and he hadn't let her.

She shrugged. "Somewhere."

He was pretty sure from the pink sweeping into her cheeks that she was fibbing about her uncertainty of the diamond's whereabouts.

"Okay," Mitzy admitted, throwing up her hands in defeat, "I know exactly where it is, in the jewelry box it came in, in the middle of my lingerie drawer, at the bottom of a stack of camisoles."

That was oddly specific for something she claimed not to care about. "Why there?" he asked curiously.

Not to let the delicious Tex-Mex food go to waste, she helped him pack up, turning her back to him in the process.

"I don't know," she muttered temperamentally, giving him a great view of her delicious backside and sleek thighs in the process.

Her lower lips slid out in a petulant pout. "I figured it would be safe. I wouldn't have to look at it every day, or… I don't know." She whirled around and glared at him in exasperation. "I just never got around to going to the jeweler to see if they would buy it back, okay?"

And if he believed that, she probably also had swampland to sell him.

He shut the lid on the cooler and left everything else as it was. He moved toward her with lazy deliberation. "So," he surmised with a taunting smile, as he took her resisting body all the way in his arms, "if truth be told, I was correct. You're still as stuck on me as I always have been on you."

Silence fell.

As it faded, so did her resistance.

Mitzy let out a long sigh. She looked at him, still petulant. "As much as I hate to admit it, cowboy, apparently so."

Chuckling, he lowered his head and gave her the kind of kiss that let her know whether she wanted to admit it or not she was still his woman and he was her man. End of story.

He sifted his hands through her hair. Glad her ambivalence hadn't lasted nearly as long this time. "So we're good?" he asked thickly.

Mitzy released a long breath. "Secretly, yes," she admitted, reluctantly relaxing in his arms, "we're good."

"But…?" He sensed conditions he wouldn't like coming on.

She extricated herself and went to find her coat. "I don't want anyone to know we're even thinking about picking up where we left off, at least not yet. I don't want that kind of interest or pressure."

He could understand her not wanting her mother involved in the situation just yet.

After all, Judith could be a handful. Even with the easy-going Walter there to run interference.

As for the rest…

Hating to be the bearer of bad news, Chase said, "Actually, sweetheart, as far as the interest goes, I think that horse already left the corral."

She went very still. Her eyes held his. "What do you mean?" she asked with trepidation.

Chase figured he might as well spit it out. "My brother Jack told me people in Laramie are already taking bets on how long it will be until we're actually married."

She paled. "You're kidding."

He wished.

Pressure, of any kind, of any degree, from any place, would not help him win Mitzy's heart. In fact, it would have the opposite effect.

She came nearer, brows raised. "Did you place a bet?"

"Nope." Although Chase knew what he privately *hoped* would happen. "I don't want to jinx anything," he said with absolute honesty.

Mitzy groaned in distress. "I don't, either. At least," she clarified, as they headed out the door, en route to relieve their two volunteer babysitters by 6:00 p.m., "we're on the same page about this."

They were.

It was what to do about their feelings that they couldn't agree on. Mitzy wanted to hide, and as much as he hated it, Chase understood why. Her parents' divorce and her mother's subsequent remarriages—save the one to the beloved Walter—had not been exactly encouraging to Mitzy. Whereas his folks' relationship stood as a beacon to all that was good and enduring, when it came to formal legal unions.

Bottom line: he wanted the kind of solid, loving, everlasting marriage his parents had.

Mitzy, on the other hand, preferred to keep one foot out the door when it came to romance.

No doubt she felt not being tied down would keep her safe. It was going to be up to him to show her just the opposite was true. For both their sakes, he would work on that.

He doubted he would be able to get that done before they left for Dallas, for the quads' debut, on Saturday. But maybe, if he were persistent and persuasive enough, he would be able to achieve success before Christmas.

As it happened, Mitzy and Chase weren't able to see each other at all on Thursday. Chase was tied up, arranging financials for a struggling business he was attempting to purchase before year's end. Whereas Mitzy was working on the details of the MCS Christmas party to take place the following weekend.

The time apart gave her some much-needed time to think.

She realized she'd been a little too emotional the day before when Chase had arranged for their trip down memory lane.

For her, that time was as fraught with unhappy memories as happy ones.

Chase viewed it differently. Seemingly through a rose-colored lens.

The point was, the past was over. The future was too far ahead to think about. All they really had was the present, and in the present, she was really enjoying spending time with Chase again.

She no longer wanted a closure that would end things.

Neither did he.

So maybe for now, with the complicated holidays coming up, they should concentrate on that.

Which was exactly what she did when Chase was able to come by as per usual on Friday evening.

"It looks like we're going to have a good crowd at the company Christmas party," she told him excitedly soon after he arrived. She took his coat and hung it up in the hall closet. "It seems like all the employees are coming and bringing family and or a friend with them." She made a face as she relayed, "The only problem is the potato salad. We have more people wanting to make that than any of the other side dishes."

He returned her hello hug and kiss then walked with her to the family room, where the quads were all snoozing away. He took a peek at each of them, tenderness softening the strong features of his handsome face. Turning back to her, he caught her hand and tugged her down onto the sofa beside him. "What's the main entrée going to be?"

Mitzy snuggled into the curve of his arm. "Barbecue—from Sonny's. Traditionally, the company supplies that, and I've already placed the order."

He stroked a thumb over her cheek. "You could have the restaurant make the sides, too. I'd be happy to treat."

She gazed up at him, appreciative of his generosity. "Thank you, but no. You're my guest."

He grinned, appearing as happy about that as she was. Even though, she'd made it perfectly clear, he was only going as an old family friend, not her actual date.

"Besides, it's tradition that everyone brings something homemade. I'll just have to put out the call for more variety in sides, and the desserts."

He looked at the lists and gift catalogs spread out over the coffee table. "What's all this?"

Mitzy sighed. "I'm still trying to decide on the presents for the boys. Mother has already gotten them every toy for their age group. Her theory being that just because they were all born on the same day doesn't mean they should get any less than she would have given them had they been a year apart."

"So she's cornered the market on toys for the under-one set."

"Pretty much. Anyway, I was thinking. They haven't gotten any loveys yet. And they really are at that age where they might start to need them. So I was going to get each one of them a special baby blanket, embroidered with their name, and a special stuffed animal, too."

Chase nodded. "Nice."

Mitzy frowned. "But then I got stuck."

Chase's brow furrowed. "How come?"

Happy to talk this out with him—since he was the masculine influence in their lives and might, someday in the distant future, be even more if the fates allowed—Mitzy thumbed through the catalog to show him the possibilities.

"Should I go with wild animal stuffed toys, like zebras and bears, tigers and lions? Or farm animals like horses and cows and pigs and donkeys?"

Excited about the quads' very first Christmas, she rushed on, "Dinosaurs seem really popular, especially for little boys, but are those too scary? Or is it better to go with something like puppies and kittens and bunnies?" Chase's gaze widened. "As you can see, they are all adorable."

He snuggled next to her on the sofa. "They are."

"So what do you think?"

He studied her, seeming surprised that she had wanted his opinion on something this intimate and important. Finally, he said, "If it were me, I would go with different kinds of dogs and choose different breeds for each child.

Golden retriever. Black Labrador. Husky. Maybe a Bernese mountain dog." He shrugged, pointing at the pictures on the page. "They're all cute. And distinctive looking."

Mitzy had known Chase would have the answer. She hugged him exuberantly. "I like that idea."

Now all he had to do was help her decide.

They spent the next hour poring over the choices.

Mitzy put the items in her shopping cart, set the delivery for the following Monday and checked out. Relieved to have that over with, she rose and stretched, putting her hands over her head. "Now all I have to do is order the blankets and take them over to get them embroidered. Which I can do after we get back from Dallas."

Chase stood, too. Stepping behind her, he massaged the taut muscles of her shoulders and the back of her neck. Pleasure sifted through Mitzy. Chase could always make her feel so good. She had really missed having him around. Not just yesterday, but for the last ten years.

As if sensing the change in her mood, Chase turned her to face him. "Speaking of the big D..." He gently surveyed her face. "Are you-all ready for the trip tomorrow morning?"

Mitzy wasn't sure how to answer that. Embarking on the first road trip with the quadruplets was one thing. Facing her mother—and whatever secrets and potential suitors Judith had up her sleeve—definitely another.

But there was no use borrowing trouble.

Which would come soon enough.

So Mitzy concentrated on the positive. "Bridgett, Bess and Lulu were all here this afternoon, and they helped me pack. So yes, except for the things that have to go into the diaper bag last minute, we're all ready."

"Still want me to be here at the crack of dawn?"

Mitzy wished she could invite him to stay the night. But

if he did, they'd end up making love again, and neither of them would get any sleep.

Figuring they could make up for lost time later, she said, "Yes. I promised Mother we'd be at her home in Preston Hollow no later than ten."

Chase kissed the back of her hand. "Nervous?" he asked softly.

"Not as much as I would be if you weren't going to be there with us."

Chase wrapped her in his arms. "It'll all be okay," he promised.

Mitzy drew a breath. She certainly hoped so.

Chapter Ten

Judith met them at the door of her mansion, late Saturday morning. *"What happened?"* she asked, aghast.

Chase turned to Mitzy, figuring she should answer, since she had just endured the road trip from hell with her quadruplets.

Mitzy grimaced. "Turns out that being in the car more than thirty minutes or so makes them all spit up."

Or at least it had that morning, Chase thought.

Judith, who'd been about to reach out to hug them, stepped back, hands up as if to stave them off. "I'm sorry, but you-all *reek*!"

Mitzy—who had predicted this reaction from her mother—sent Chase a beleaguered glance. Then, like Chase, still holding an infant carrier with a sleeping baby in each hand, retorted with laudable calm, "We're aware we all smell like sour milk, Mother. Which is why we'd like to get everyone cleaned up, and the interior of my SUV detailed, as soon as possible."

Judith bypassed the caterers setting up and led them toward the sweeping staircase that dominated the grand entry hall of the ten-thousand-square-foot mansion. "Well, the stylists are waiting. The photographer is here." She motioned to the four young women gathered on the second-floor balcony. The childcare workers headed down en masse. Looking even more stressed, Judith turned back, fretting, "I wish you hadn't insisted on doing everything all in one day!"

Mitzy, well accustomed to her mother's griping, countered just as implacably, "We're here now. So do you want to argue about it or get going?" The nannies each took one baby boy.

Judith swept into drill-sergeant mode. "The first order of business is to get everyone out of those horrible clothes and get the vomit smell washed off." She turned to Mitzy. "I'll send someone out for the bags while you show Chase to the blue suite. And we'll have your SUV taken to the car wash."

Chase handed over the vehicle keys. "Thanks, Judith."

Walter appeared, in a polo shirt and khakis. He looked completely unfazed by all the activity swirling about them. "When you're done, come out to the pool. We'll see about getting you some refreshments…"

Glad he'd thought to bring a couple of extra shirts and jeans, Chase changed and washed up. He could hear the stylists, makeup and hair crew jockeying for top dog status as he passed Mitzy's room.

Thinking it was going to be a men's only get-together, he was surprised to see Walter *and* Judith waiting for him at one of the umbrella tables.

"I don't know how long we'll have to talk privately," Mitzy's mother began, her voice as sunny and unseason-

g red gown, its demure jewel-collared
-length hem belying the completely bare

d beautiful shoulders. Creamy satin skin.
eup, her hair upswept, diamonds glitter-
and earlobes, she looked as elegant as she
ante days.

, he was pretty damn sure, ticked off at
eaking privately with her mother and step-
two of them?

d had any choice but to be polite.

dith said, suddenly at his side. "It's time."

ing her coded message, Chase exhaled.
Judith had asked him to do this.

n Mitzy wasn't around.

drink aside, trying to get in the spirit.
e asked genially.

me is in the powder room, just off the garage.
done, you'll need to wait for my signal. I'll
our cell. Then wait for the musical cue, and
ugh the front door."

ration just got better than ever.

dded and meandered in the direction he'd been
The one good thing about having been engaged
ce upon a time was that he was as familiar with
n as he was his own parents' home.

later, he slipped out the back and walked
front. The night was getting colder. Holiday
nkled. Stars gleamed in the velvety night sky
The faint scent of wood smoke, from the home's
nstairs fireplaces, filled the air.

ack beside him, he waited.

aited.

aited.

ably warm as the December weather outside, "so I'll get straight to the point."

She poured them each a cup of peppermint tea. "Gus didn't just talk privately to you before he died, Chase. He talked to me and Walter, too."

She waited for Chase to take a sip of the fragrant beverage. "We know what you promised him. What I can't comprehend is what's taking so long!" She paused to give him a look of reproof and leaned toward him. "Why haven't you found a buyer yet for MCS? Or better yet, purchased it yourself, for McCabe Leather Goods?"

As long as they were putting all the cards on the table…

Chase straightened. "Because I also promised Gus that I would give Mitzy time to come to grips with the fact that she's not equipped to run a company like that."

"But you're doing something about it now…" Walter guessed approvingly, one businessman to another.

If only it were that simple. But, with Mitzy's heart involved, it wasn't easy. "I'm trying."

Judith scoffed. "By romancing her? And don't deny it, Chase. I have my sources. I know you've been there practically every day." She used her fingers to make quotation marks. "Helping out."

How much to tell without really making Mitzy mad? That was the question. Chase slowly exhaled. "I never stopped caring about her."

Or, it would appear, she about me…

Judith shook her head, sadness and frustration coming into her eyes. "You should have married her ten years ago. No matter what she said."

If there was such a thing as a do-over, he would be first in line. "I agree. I was a fool." *We both were.* "I'm not anymore. Believe it or not—" he looked at both Judith and Walter "—I have a handle on this."

It was a delicate process, one that could easily blow up in their faces. But he was going to proceed carefully. Bring her around, one step at a time. Just the way Gus had wanted. "I have a handle on her and the whole situation."

Judith squinted slightly as if to signal him.

For what, Chase didn't know.

He soon found out as a shadow loomed over them.

Mitzy approached, a stressed-out look on her face. Her hair was already in curlers and she had makeup suitable for studio photography on—which meant way too much. She was wearing some sort of kimono robe and slippers, and she looked more miserable than he had ever seen her. Had she overheard what they'd been talking about? It was impossible to tell. She padded closer, arms crossed militantly in front of her. "Mother, please don't put pressure on him."

Maybe not, Chase thought with relief.

Maybe she just assumed her mother was meddling, as per usual.

Judith tossed her head. "I'm not going to be shy about saying what I feel about all this, Mitzy."

Had she ever been? Chase wondered.

Mitzy lifted a brow, daring her mother to go on.

And of course, Judith did. "Chase might not have been right for you before, since he hadn't yet made his fortune. Now that he has, he should capitalize on that success. Marry you. Adopt the boys. And move you and the babies back to Dallas for good."

Mitzy's demeanor got even icier. She glared at her mother. "Or not."

Figuring no good could come of continuing this conversation, Chase jumped in, half rising out of his chair. "Did you need some help with something, sweetheart?"

She gave him a long look that could have meant any

number of thi
oted back to Ju
say this, I do n
a mess… My st
anything and I a

"Not to worry
The two wome
Chase couldn'
be starting to lean
tle. Which would b
needed each other n

Walter pushed his
that." He helped hims
ies on the plate. "I to
cially not today, but sh
handling this first Chri
she wants everyone to t

Funny, Chase had jus
He turned back to th
stepfather-in-law. "Is it
Mitzy to a number of elig

Walter gave a half shru
aware as everyone else that
intentioned, don't always w
a backup plan…"

One, Chase realized, his
clude him.

Chase thought his days of f
had passed. Apparently not. It w
taking Mitzy around. Introduc
after another. All wealthy. Succ

All incredibly interested in M
And why not? He'd never seen

in a body-clingir
neckline and knee
back.

Damn, she ha
In the subtle ma
ing at her throat
had in her debut

She was also
him. For even s
father about the

Not that he'
"Chase," Ju
Understand
Of course,
Again, whe
He put hi
"Where…?"

"The costu
When you're
text you on y
come in thro

This cele
Chase no
instructed.
to Mitzy on
this mansi

Minute
around the
lights twi
overhead.
many do
Knaps
And w
And

Finally, his cell phone dinged. He looked at the screen. The message from Judith said, MAKE YOUR ENTRANCE! And don't forget to be jolly!

Chase shook his head.

As if he could.

Telling himself it was for Mitzy and the kids, he headed in.

Mitzy stood at the top of the grand staircase. Her feet were killing her. She hadn't worn heels in forever. And certainly not five-inch designer instruments of torture.

Her dress, though dazzling, was equally uncomfortable. For one thing, her back was cold from waist to shoulders. Her front felt hot. And now—to make her attention-loving mother happy—she had to make like a supermodel in front of two hundred and fifty–plus guests.

She only hoped her boys behaved...

Down below, the small group of musicians abruptly stopped playing. Judith and Walter moved to the center of the grand entry hall. "Welcome, everyone!" Judith said cheerfully. "And merry Christmas to one and all! I know you-all have been waiting to meet our new grandsons... so without further ado, Mitzy darling, come on down!"

A smile plastered on her face, Mitzy gracefully led the way. Behind her, the four young nannies—all dressed like elves—descended with her infants.

She was nearly at the bottom when the front door opened with a flourish.

A very tall, surprisingly buff, Santa strode in. Apparently, Santa had forgotten his pillow. Or eschewed it altogether.

"Ho, ho, ho!" boomed a very familiar voice.

Oh, no, Mitzy thought, her pique at Chase fading.

Her mother hadn't...

She had.

"Santa" strode toward her. Dropped his knapsack at her feet. "Who do we have here?" he thundered, hands on his hips, looking down at Mitzy.

Like he didn't know.

Without warning, he put his hand around her waist, bent her backward from the waist. She clung to his shoulders. "Could it be," Santa continued asking heartily, "the potential Mrs. Claus?"

Laughter erupted as Saint Nick stole a short, sweet, thoroughly mesmerizing kiss. Whoops and hollers followed. Mitzy could imagine the expression on her mother's face.

Hers felt like it was going bright pink.

"Santa," she warned, looking deep into his merry gray-blue eyes.

Chase cocked a hand to his ear. "What was that?" he said, even louder, to the amusement of all those around her. "Oh!" He slapped a hand across his heart. "Why certainly I'll kiss you again!" He tugged off his beard, still holding her bent over backward from the waist. Her weight resting on one of his rock-hard thighs, he lowered his mouth to hers. And this time, without the pesky beard between them, it was, Mitzy realized, going to be a real kiss. The kind that had her world spinning…

She had time to prevent it, of course. She could have turned her head to the side or evaded the smooch any number of ways. But she didn't because she also knew that ignoring the growing feelings between them was not what she wanted at all.

For too long she had denied caring about him. Wanting him. Coveting a life with him.

So when he lowered his lips to hers, she opened her mouth to his and returned his kiss, deeply, passionately. It didn't matter that he was publicly stamping her as his.

Yearning swept through her, overwhelming her heart and her mind. She wrapped her arms around him, drawing him closer. Her soft curves fit against the hard warmth of his chest. She loved the sexy male scent of him. The womanly way he made her feel.

She loved that he wasn't afraid to show how he felt, either. Once again, she found herself needing and wanting Chase the way she had never wanted and needed anyone else.

Had they been alone, they definitely would have made love again. Even if she was still a tiny bit ticked off at him.

But they weren't.

So…

She let the kiss come to an end.

He slowly brought her upright, his adoring gaze lingering on her face before returning ever so slowly to her eyes.

Her heart did a little flip in her chest.

She didn't know why she felt so happy she was close to bursting into tears, but she did.

His smile turned tender, his glance direct.

He put the beard back on and turned to Mitzy's four sons, who were cuddled contentedly in their nannies' arms. "Ho, ho, ho," he said in a baby-friendly tone. "Hello, Joe. Zach. Alex. Gabe." He greeted each with a smile and a very tender kiss—the kind he usually bestowed on them when he said good-night or goodbye. "Have you boys been good this year? I think you have. I think you've been very, very good."

Judith came up beside Mitzy, her smile frozen in place. "I'm going to kill that man of yours." Mitzy's mother pushed the words through gritted teeth.

Which, Mitzy thought, *almost* made the impromptu kisses worth it.

If she weren't so quietly ticked off at him, that was.

* * *

The next two hours were busy ones, with the nannies taking the babies around so Judith and Walter could show them off. Mitzy and Chase—who had changed back into his own evening attire—took over the task of greeting all of the guests. When it was time for the boys' next feeding and changing, the nannies swept them off upstairs to the mansion's east wing.

Mitzy followed. Wanting to be there if she was needed. She wasn't.

So she went back into the hall, where Chase was waiting, hands shoved into the pockets of his trousers. He had the same look on his face he'd had before they had launched into the explosive, emotional argument that had ended their engagement. The kind of look that said he knew she wasn't going to like whatever it was that he had done, when he told her about it, but felt 100 percent justified in his actions just the same. And worse, expected her to accept his disloyalty and bullheadedness just the same.

Only this time, her mother and Walter were somehow involved in whatever was going on, too.

"They set up the buffet," he said casually.

Mitzy wasn't sure she could do much more pretending. Especially when she felt this betrayed. "I'm sure it's very lavish," she returned with studied politeness. "Why don't you go fix yourself a plate?"

His gaze narrowed. "Why don't we both go help ourselves to some dinner?"

There was no doubt about it. He was feeling guilty and uncomfortable about something.

Mitzy jerked in a bolstering breath. "I wanted to get some air first."

He nodded as if accepting the time to clear the air between them had come. "I'll go with you."

Knowing the gardens would be chilly, she ducked into her room to get a white cashmere evening wrap. They traversed the backstairs, walked through the kitchen. Chase grabbed two glasses of champagne and followed her past the sea of caterers out the back door. They moved away from the house, from the sounds of music and laughter.

"You're pissed off at me," Chase said as they reached the gazebo, the one place that would afford them some privacy.

Mitzy's heart pounded at the notion that their relationship could be ruined. Again. She tilted her head at him, determined to learn the truth. Even if it smashed her heart to smithereens. "What was it you said, out by the pool?" she quoted with devastating softness. "'I have a handle on her. And the whole situation…'"

Chapter Eleven

Regret sifted through him. "How much did you hear?" Chase asked.

Mitzy looked at him, a mixture of temper and resentment simmering in her pretty aquamarine eyes. "If I say 'everything' versus 'not much,' will it change your answer?"

Secrets were bad news. He had always known this. "I didn't ask to be put in the middle of this."

She set her cell phone and glass of champagne down with a great show of irritation, then turned back to him, the hem of her dress swirling around her showgirl-fine legs. "Keep going."

He set his glass down, too, and stepped toward her, determined to see out his responsibility. "Your dad called me before he died, and asked me to meet him at the hospital. He had just learned that he was terminal and wasn't expected to live out the spring."

Grief drained the color from her face. "And he didn't," she whispered, tearing up. "He died in May."

Forcing himself to be as strong as she needed him to be, Chase closed the distance remaining between them. He took her in his arms and continued to hold her, despite her mute resistance. "Gus wanted to make sure that you were protected."

Mitzy inhaled sharply, the soft luscious curves of her breasts rising against the shimmering fabric of her red dress.

Chase pushed his reaction away. Gazing frankly down at her, he continued, "Your dad told me he had tried to talk to you about the business, about selling it even before he died, since that—along with your small general welfare trust he had set up when you were a kid, and his house—was going to be your inheritance. But you were adamant that his legacy be continued, that you could run MCS in his absence."

Mitzy flattened a hand over Chase's chest and pushed him away.

Resolutely, Chase went on. "He said he knew that you equated giving up MCS with giving up on life."

Mitzy gripped both ends of her white cashmere evening wrap. "With good reason," she retorted fiercely, lifting her chin. "MCS was the only thing that kept him going that last year."

Chase watched her go back to get her glass. Her graceful strides were as mesmerizingly feminine as the rest of her. It was all he could do to keep from making love to her again, then and there.

But sensing she needed more from him than that right now…a hell of a lot more…he walked over to get his glass, too. Reminding gently but firmly, "That's not true, Mitzy."

She stopped in midsip.

"It wasn't the company he lived for. *You* were what kept him going." Dammit, now he was getting choked up, too. "Your dad loved you more than anything. And because he did, he wanted to make things as easy as he could on you after he passed."

Chase quaffed half his glass. Resolved to give her the support she needed, he looked her in the eye and continued seriously, "So your dad asked me to quietly watch over you, from afar, and to buy the business from you, when the time was right, preferably before the end of the year."

Mitzy moved to one of the stone benches. She started to sit down on it, then stopped, and spread out her wrap first. Looking as if her knees would no longer support her, she settled on the bench in thoughtful silence. "That's why you came to see me before Thanksgiving."

The promise to Gus had been only part of it. Sensing she wasn't ready to hear that, though, Chase merely nodded.

He sat down beside her and took her hand in his. "Gus knew it was going to be tough on you to let MCS go. He thought, given a little time and effort, that I could convince you it was the right thing."

"So all this," Mitzy said, jumping to her feet once again. "You coming by nightly…helping me with the boys…even coming with us to Dallas for all this ridiculous pageantry tonight," she cried, *"was all a means to an end?"*

Chase figured there was no reason to pretend otherwise. "You're damn right it was," he said gruffly, taking her all the way into his arms. He smoothed the hair from her cheek and looked down into her face.

She blinked in astonishment. Obviously not used to such gut-wrenching honesty.

Loving the warmth and softness of her as much as he loved the way she looked in that pretty shimmery cocktail dress, he brought her closer still. She surged against him as their bodies merged, and everything that had been wrong between them righted. He shook his head, finally pushed to admit just how much he wanted her, had always needed her. "How else was I going to find my way back into your heart and your life?"

He lowered his mouth to hers and gave her a full-on kiss, filled with everything he felt, everything he had suppressed. She gasped in surprise, caution mingling with the yearning in her gaze. "Chase…"

He grazed her earlobe with his teeth, touched his mouth to her throat, her cheek, her temple, before once again moving to her lips. And this time, when he fit his lips over hers, she was ready for him. She made a sexy little murmur in the back of her throat, and then her hands were coming up to cup his head. She opened her mouth to allow him deeper, wider access and rose on tiptoe, pressing her breasts against his chest, her thighs against his…

Mitzy had meant to read him the riot act, not kiss him, but now that she was in his arms again, she couldn't think of any place she would rather be. It wasn't so much the soft, sure feel of his mouth over hers. Although that was tantalizing. Or the way his tongue dallied provocatively with hers, finding every sweet spot with ease.

It was the way he constantly took charge and dominated the moment, and her. She might not need his protection, but she welcomed it. Just as she welcomed the notion that she was no longer meant to go through this life constantly strong, fiercely independent. Alone.

She could lean on someone.

She could lean on him.

She wanted to lean on him. To the point, who knew what might have happened next had it not been for the insistent ping of her cell phone.

Chase immediately halted the kiss. The amazing intimacy ended. She felt stunned and elated, bereft and confused. With a stifled oath, she broke away, went to retrieve her still-pinging phone and read the text message on screen. Oh, no. She whirled back to Chase, in full Mommy Mode. Grasping her wrap and half-empty glass, she said, "I'm needed upstairs. Right now."

Chase went with her and, for once, Mitzy did not try to dissuade his assistance. He was as good with her four boys as she was, and it sounded like the little ones needed them both.

Mitzy rushed into the second-floor hallway of the mansion's east wing, where all four nannies and the babies were waiting. She took in the red tear-streaked faces and heartrending howls of distress. Her heart ached. "How long have they been crying like this?"

All four nannies talked at once. "Since shortly after you left. We gave them all bottles, which they drank, but they absolutely refuse to be put down. They don't want to be rocked. Or held. Or walked around."

"Well, no wonder," Mitzy said, gazing around at the four separate "nurseries" that had been set up in four different guest rooms. She reached for Joe, who was crying the hardest, and then Gabe, who had big fat tears running down his chubby little face.

Chase stepped in to take Zach, who for once was not the least bit calm, and then Alex, who'd been trying to twist himself out of his nanny's arms.

"What happened to the temporary setup in the playroom?" That she had personally supervised?

"Judith ordered it all disassembled and put away when the party started. She wanted the boys sleeping in regular cribs, not Pack 'n Plays."

Mitzy gaped. "But the cribs are all in different bedrooms!"

"Judith felt it would be better if they didn't disturb each other."

Oh, Mother, Mitzy thought, distressed. *You may have meant well, but...*

With as much patience as she could muster, Mitzy explained, "The boys need to see each other to feel safe." The same way they needed to be held by her and Chase now.

"That didn't help before you got here," Nanny Gwen said.

Mitzy looked over at Chase, who appeared as concerned as she felt. She had never been more glad to have his strong, steady presence. "Where are the Pack 'n Plays now?" she asked.

Nanny Belinda shrugged. "I don't know. The storage room in the attic, I think."

Mitzy groaned. That was at the other end of the mansion, on the fourth floor.

"Do you want me to go and retrieve them?" Chase offered.

Mitzy shook her head.

He looked around, considering. "I could try to disassemble three of the four cribs and put them all in one room."

A task like that would require tools and take hours.

Again, Mitzy shook her head. "I want to take them home. Now," she said.

Chase did a double take. "You want to drive all the way back to Laramie."

So much.

Mitzy edged close enough to inhale his brisk soap-and-man scent. She looked up at him persuasively. "It's just a little after nine. If we leave now, we could be back by midnight."

"And if they get carsick again?"

"We'll deal with it, the same way we dealt with it this morning." The most important thing was getting them home, where they felt safe and secure.

He wanted to go, too. She could see it in his expression. Still, he hesitated. Mitzy guessed what was bothering him. "We're not going to be able to attend any more of the party if we want the boys to stay calm."

Chase's brow furrowed. "Your mother…"

"Is just going to have to understand. Besides, her soiree is going to go on until at least two a.m. If not later. So it's not like she would be spending all that much time with her grandchildren. Or us."

"She'll be upset," Chase predicted.

"I know." Mitzy sighed.

But right now she was more concerned about the comfort and emotional security of her four boys.

Mitzy turned to the four nannies, who were unfortunately still dressed like elves at her mother's request. "Would you-all mind helping us get everything out the staff entrance, to my SUV? And then you-all will be able to leave."

Nanny Gwen looked all the more worried. "You don't want us to say anything to Judith or Walter?"

"No. I'll take care of that after we're on the road." Mitzy paused momentarily to direct the packing up, as did Chase. Finished, they moved in tandem down the back stairs. "…I promise you. You'll get your full fee and won't be blamed for this."

Fifteen minutes later, the boys were safely strapped into their car seats, the luggage was loaded and they had a to-go meal of finger foods from the caterers in their possession.

Chase climbed behind the wheel, while Mitzy elected to take the center place in the middle row of her eight-passenger SUV, where, if need be, she could reach the two babies beside her, and the two infants in back of her, too.

Uniformed valets moved the cars that were in the way.

Chase put on some soothing Christmas music and drove sedately through the elegant neighborhood. By the time they neared the highway, all four boys were fast asleep.

For the first time in hours, Mitzy relaxed.

Aware she was starving, and he had to be, too, she opened up the yuletide feast that had been packed for them. "We've got country ham biscuits with cranberry marmalade."

"Sounds good."

Aware how domestic—and comfortable—this all suddenly was, she reached across the back of the driver's seat and handed one to him. Her forearm nudged his broad shoulder in the process.

Warmth filtered through her at the brief contact.

She savored the sensation. "And beef tenderloin on sourdough with horseradish."

Their fingers brushed again. He downed the finger food in two bites. "Also delicious."

And on they went, with Mitzy handing across various finger sandwiches, cookies and tarts.

Finished, and feeling much better, now that at least one of her appetites was sated, she opened up a bottle of chilled water and handed that to him, too.

He glanced at her over his shoulder. "Thanks, darlin'."

His low gravelly voice was intensely sexy. It reminded her of the kisses they had shared in the gazebo, and the intensely physical longing that welled up within her whenever they were alone.

Mitzy tugged the hem of her skirt over her knees and

settled more comfortably in her seat. "Actually, I should be saying that to you. It's been quite a day and it's not over yet."

He shrugged, his broad shoulders flexing against the starched fabric of his shirt. His jacket lay on the seat next to him. "We'll be back in Laramie in another hour."

Mitzy glanced at the sweet cherubic faces of her children, thought of how much they meant to her, and were coming to mean to Chase, too. "Hopefully, they'll continue sleeping."

He turned his head in her direction, giving her a brief view of his handsome profile. "At least they're not spitting up."

Mitzy chuckled, as he meant her to. "Amen to that," she said with heartfelt emotion. The trip to Dallas had been horrendous! But Chase had taken the calamity in stride, as always. A fact that showed yet again what a good daddy he was going to be someday. Husband, too...

Hers, maybe?

Or was she getting way, way ahead of herself here?

As the pensive silence continued, he caught her glance in the rearview mirror. Briefly, tenderness and an understanding that seemed to go soul deep reverberated between them. "You doing okay?"

Yes. And no. Maybe because whenever they were together like this, she found herself wanting to erase the years they had spent apart, and simply pick up where they left off. Madly in love and about to get married.

And how foolish was that? Given the things, like their attitudes about business and succeeding at all costs, that still kept them apart?

"Mitzy?" he pressed softly. "Are you doing all right?"

Aware her insides were suddenly trembling, she took a deep energizing breath. "In what sense?" *In the sense*

*that although I know you still desire me and like hanging
out with me, and my boys, but that I don't know if you will
ever love me again? Or if you ever really did?*

What if it had all been infatuation on his part, then and
now? She knew how *she* felt, but was that enough to build
a family on?

Oblivious to the real reason behind her uncertainty, he
prodded in concern, "About what we talked about in the
gazebo."

So many questions. So many answers she wasn't sure
she wanted to know. Deciding there was no better time to
finish hashing this issue out, she replied, "What did my
mother and Walter have to do with everything that's happened the last few weeks?"

His hands gripping the wheel, he exhaled roughly. "I
thought I was the only one who knew about the promise
I made to Gus. But today, out by the pool, I learned that
Judith and Walter knew, too."

Mitzy took a moment to absorb that. "You were
shocked?"

"Speechless."

It wasn't all that hard to imagine the rest of the pool-
side conversation. Mitzy shook her head in bemusement,
guessing, "My mother wants you to get on with the purchase of Martin Custom Saddle, whether it is done by you
or someone else." She jerked in a breath, pushed on. "So
she was pressuring you. And you told her you were handling it. And me."

"Bingo. Although," Chase added wryly, "I'm not sure
the latter is quite true. Since no one really 'handles' you,
Mitzy Martin."

She laughed, as he meant her to. "True."

"I understand where your mom's coming from, though."
Chase turned onto the farm-to-market road that led straight

to Laramie. "She wants you to have less extraneous stuff
to deal with right now, given the fact you have four sons to
raise on your own."

It was a lot, Mitzy admitted. Except it didn't seem like
so much when Chase was by her side. Then it all seemed
quite manageable.

"And you…?" she asked, more curious than ever about
what her ex was thinking and feeling. "What do you want,
Chase?"

Once again, he caught her glance briefly in the mirror.
The corners of his sensual lips turned up enticingly. "I
want you to be happy, too," he said sincerely.

The question was, where did her happiness lie?

With the boys? With Chase? With the family business?
Or some combination of all three?

They arrived home at midnight, just as Mitzy had predicted they would. The boys woke long enough to get their
diapers changed, sleep suits on, bottles of formula emptied.

Chase burped them. Mitzy swaddled.

By twelve thirty all were fast asleep again in their cribs.

"What a day," Chase whispered, squeezing her hand,
as the two of them paused next to the four cribs for one
last long, loving look.

Mitzy shook her head in overwhelming affection that
included the tall, handsome man beside her, too. "No kidding," she whispered back.

Together, they eased out of the nursery. Aware she must
look ridiculous in her shimmery red evening gown and favorite fluffy spa slippers, Mitzy turned to him. He looked
incredibly dapper in his starched white shirt and dark trousers. His tie was long gone. The collar of his shirt was
open, sleeves rolled up partway to the elbow. He looked
sexy and disheveled, and ardent as all get-out.

His gaze drifted over her, pausing on her lips before returning with slow deliberation to her eyes. The desire she'd felt earlier came roaring back.

And, if the dark hue of his smoky-blue eyes was any indication, he was feeling mighty amorous, too.

"Nevertheless, I think we managed the bedtime routine in record time," he murmured. He caught her hand and pulled her against him in the upstairs hall. One hand drifted lazily down her spine, eliciting tingles of warmth. The other tucked a strand of hair behind her ear.

"So," he said, his gaze roving over her before returning ever so slowly to her lips. Then her eyes. "Kicking me out?"

Mitzy inhaled the familiar soap-and-man scent of him. Beneath that, the lingering hint of his masculine cologne. She knew if she wanted to keep her heart intact she should do just that.

She also knew it had been a very long time since she had felt this close to him. Her bedroom was just steps away. The fragrant scent of evergreen added to the magic of Christmas in the air. And what was this season about, really, but giving. And she had so much she wanted to give to him.

Realizing there was only one way to figure out how he felt about her, too, Mitzy wound her arms around his neck. Allowing her heart to guide her, she leaned up, threading her fingers through his hair, guiding his lips down to hers as she looked into his eyes and whispered, "Not unless you really want to go…"

"I don't."

Yearning spiraled through her as he moved his hands over her shoulders, down her spine, to her hips. He pressed her against him, so she could feel how much he wanted her. Their lips met in a melding of heat and need. She kissed him back, sweetly, deeply. Tingles surged through her, tautening her nipples, pooling low in her tummy. Damn but she wanted him. So very much.

And still they kissed and kissed, the feel of his mouth on hers filling her with the kind of love and tenderness she had wanted all her life. An emotion that was so much more than what they had shared before.

He tunneled his hands through her hair for a moment, breathing hard, resting his forehead against hers. "But I want you to be sure…"

"Then stay." She kissed him again, aware it was past time they took this most important next step. "The entire night…"

He let out a low growl of assent. Still kissing her, danced her backward into the master, all the way to her bed. She turned on the twinkling lights still strewn across the headboard. Kicked off her slippers and pulled him flush against her, opening her lips to the investigating pleasure of his. His hands cupped her breasts through the thin fabric of her dress and he kissed her again, a deep, giving kiss that had her entire body going soft with yearning, senses spinning, heart soaring.

She undid the buttons on his shirt while he released the zipper at her spine. Her dress was eased off. His shirt, too. Chase grinned as both garments fell to the ground.

He admired the curves spilling out of the lacy décolletage of her bra, the gentle slope of her tummy, the angle of her hips. "You are so beautiful," he whispered.

"You, too, cowboy," she said, reaching for his fly, cupping his velvety hardness with her hand.

He moaned in satisfaction, his lips forging a burning trail down the slope of her neck, across the curve of one breast, then the other. She quivered at the long sensual strokes of his tongue, the light scrape of his teeth, the soothing feel of his lips. Need spiraled—and then blossomed—deep inside her.

She guided him back to the bed, pushed him down, removed her panties and his pants, and climbed astride him.

She ran her hands across the width of his shoulders, over his chest, luxuriating in the satin smoothness of his skin, and the flex of solid muscle. Reaching over to the nightstand for a condom, she quickly sheathed him. Impatient, she lifted and positioned herself, aware nothing had ever felt as right as this.

Chase hadn't expected Mitzy would have the energy to make love after the day they'd had, but he was glad she was as hot for him as he was for her. Giving way to the primal possessiveness he felt whenever he was near her like this, he took his time, touching and tantalizing, stroking and adoring, until her head fell back and her body shuddered with pleasure.

He held her through the aftershocks. Satisfaction rumbling through him, he continued undressing her.

When they were both naked, he eased her onto her back. Found a condom and, nudging her legs apart, slid between her thighs. She gasped as his lips crossed her abdomen, forged a trail up and down her inner thighs. She surrendered even as she arched, catching his head between her hands, until the climax she'd experienced earlier came roaring back.

She moaned as he shifted over top of her. Caught her to him in the ultimate closeness. She trembled. He dove deep. And then all was lost in the incredible welling passion between them. They were pushing toward the edge. Surging, racing, feeling. Climaxing together. Floating freely. Coming back down. Holding each other. Loving. Kissing. And starting all over again.

They woke to change and feed the boys around four in the morning. When they'd all been tended to and put back to bed, Mitzy turned to Chase.

Wrapped in a white spa robe and slippers, her hair tousled, cheeks pink from sleep, she looked as delectable as ever.

He followed her down to the kitchen and watched her bypass the coffeemaker and pour them both a glass of orange juice. Mitzy tilted her head at him, intuitive as ever. "Something on your mind?"

So this was how new parents felt… Doing his best to quell his unprecedented anxiety, Chase asked, "Is everything okay with the little fellas?"

She paused, glass halfway to her lips. "Yes. Why?"

Clad in trousers and a T-shirt, Chase shrugged. "I thought they were starting to sleep through the night."

Mitzy smiled and, still sipping her juice, tucked her free hand into his. "If you call five or six hours at a time 'through the night,' then yes," she admitted, setting her empty glass aside, "they have started sleeping from midnight until nearly dawn most of the time. I imagine they didn't tonight because they're off schedule from the trip."

It was still dark outside. She looked tired and in need of cuddling. Tenderness sifting through him, Chase finished his drink and asked, "Want to go back to bed for a while?"

Mitzy yawned. "Please."

Together, they headed back to her bedroom.

Chase dropped his trousers and, clad in boxer briefs and a T-shirt, went around to get in on the other side of the bed. Then paused, his gaze drifting to the fabric-covered box she'd left on the chaise in the corner. The lid was half-off. The ribbon edge of a homecoming mum was sticking out. Recognizing his high school colors—not hers—he went back to investigate. "What's this?"

Mitzy flushed. "Just a box of old mementos."

He sat down on the chaise. "Is this the one I gave you my senior year?"

Mitzy perched on the opposite side of the chaise, facing him. The sentimental items rested between them. "You convinced me you couldn't get a date to the dance, and I needed to rescue you—as a friend, of course—so I grabbed the dress I had worn to my own dance and came into town to visit my dad."

The memory was a good one. Chase smiled nostalgically, too. "I remember you came to the football game to see me play."

"Which is where that homecoming mum comes in." A tradition in Texas, the huge corsage was decorated with two feet of satin ribbons and all sorts of bling.

Chase took the lid all the way off. "What else is in here?"

Mitzy ducked her head shyly. "Other random things."

Pleased, Chase noted, "Other random things that involve the two of us."

Movie ticket stubs, concert programs, the take-out menu from their first trip to a popular San Angelo drive-in restaurant, with their choices circled. Several mixed tapes of music he had made just for her.

And it wasn't just ancient keepsakes. Amazed, he looked at her. "The programs from the Christmas concert in the town square are even in here."

Mitzy shrugged, her eyes dancing merrily. "I needed some place to put them."

"Do you have stuff from other boyfriends, too?"

"No!" She seemed offended. "Do you keep anything to remind you of your old girlfriends?"

He shook his head, just as adamantly. "Of course not."

Her relief was as palpable as his. "Do you have anything that belonged to the two of us, when we were together?"

"No," he admitted regretfully.

She nodded and put the lid back on the box.

"Then, we broke up," he continued in an effort to explain. "So I figured maybe it was just as well I didn't have anything sentimental except our engagement photos to look at."

Hurt came and went in her aquamarine eyes. She stepped into her closet and came out a couple of minutes later wearing a pair of flannel menswear-style pajamas. "Did you keep those?" she asked, almost too casually.

He went back to what had become "his side" of her bed and climbed in. He sat up against the pillows. "I was so ticked off when you told me it was over, I tried to throw them away."

"But…?" she prodded.

Usually, he was the one hiding his feelings. Not tonight. "Every time I took the pictures out to the trash, something stopped me. I just…couldn't do it." He threw back the covers to welcome her. She came around and climbed in bed beside him.

"Lulu knew it. And offered to take custody of them for me until I decided what I wanted to do with them."

Still sitting up, her arms wrapped around her raised knees, she studied him. Her brows knit together in a frown, confirming his nagging sensation that this was dangerous territory. "And?"

Chase exhaled. "I never decided. She mentioned to me the other day that she still has them, so I guess that tells us something, too." Like Gus, his family hadn't quite given up on them, either.

"And now?" she prodded, as if much depended on his answer.

He kissed the back of her wrist, aware it was never too late to make amends. "I wish I had kept stuff from when we first got to know each other, back in high school, and we were trying to figure out how to date each other without actually dating each other." He flashed a crooked grin at the caution they had exhibited then—and now. Wrapping his arm around her shoulders, he admitted gruffly, "It would have been nice to add to the memorabilia we're collecting now."

Mitzy did a double take. She twisted around to better see his face. "What memorabilia?"

He retrieved his cell phone from the nightstand and showed her a dozen photos of her and him and the quads. "You-all are always with me."

Her eyes suddenly shimmering, Mitzy reached over and wordlessly showed him her phone, too. The screen saver on hers was the photo of the six of them, taken at the holiday concert. "You're with me, too," she admitted thickly.

Once again they were on the same path.

Hot damn. Talk about a merry Christmas!

He put both phones aside and took her in his arms, ready to give her the love she yearned for. "Speaking of memories," he proposed softly, reveling in the sweet and gentle yearning he saw in her eyes, "what do you say… let's make some new ones…"

And because it was the season, they did.

Chapter Twelve

Judith called the next morning. And as usual did not mask the faint note of disapproval in her tone. "I understand why you wanted to leave last night, darling, but I wish you had said goodbye."

Mitzy cringed, imagining the well-intentioned but misguided lecture sure to follow. She caught Chase's eye, mouthed the word *Judith*, and switched her phone to her other ear. "I wanted to, Mother, but you were busy with your guests."

Judith huffed. "I would have stepped away, Mitzy!"

Unfortunately, the situation would not have ended there. At least not the way Mitzy wanted it to be resolved. "And pressured me into staying. Or tried to, and as fussy as the quads were being," she continued gently, doing her best to make peace with her mother in the holiday season, "it wouldn't have worked. They needed to be home, in their own beds."

Judith paused, with grandmotherly concern. "Did they sleep well once they got back to Laramie?" she asked hopefully at last.

Mitzy smiled and met Chase's eyes. He looked incredibly sexy walking around her kitchen, clad in a pair of nice-fitting denim jeans and a white T-shirt.

He hadn't shaved, and his short sandy-brown hair was agreeably rumpled.

"They nodded off at midnight, woke at four, got up briefly to eat and then went back to sleep for another four hours. We just put them back down again a little while ago."

"What about the travel issues? Were they sick?"

"Not a bit," Mitzy relayed happily. "They slept the entire way home."

"Well, that's wonderful news," her mother said proudly.

Mitzy walked over to check on the babies, who were all sleeping soundly in the bassinets in the adjacent family room. She returned to the kitchen, where Chase was making coffee. And thought how much nicer it would be if she were surrounded by her entire family. "I really want you and Walter to come here for Christmas and spend it with us. Especially this year." With Dad gone. She swallowed around the ache in her throat. "Please tell me you'll think about it."

Judith paused. "Can I bring the nannies and a chef this time?"

And turn it into an increasingly extravagant, and hence, less personal, event? "No, it will be just the eight of us," Mitzy said firmly, watching Chase pull a package of bacon, a dozen eggs and a bottle of orange juice from the fridge.

"Eight?" Judith repeated quizzically.

Oh, heavens, talk about a slip of the tongue! Mitzy winced, temporizing, "Ahh... I was thinking Chase might be here at least part of the time, too. We haven't really talked about it yet."

He shrugged and said in his low, sexy baritone, "If that's an invitation, sweetheart, I'll be here."

Judith gasped. "He's still there?"

Oh, yes, Mitzy thought with a Cheshire grin, and looking *mighty* fine! "Making breakfast," she affirmed.

"I see."

Her mother probably did. Especially after that outrageously hot kiss Chase had laid on her during the party the previous evening.

Mitzy cleared her throat. "Anyway, Mother—" she turned away from Chase's frank assessing gaze "—I do appreciate everything you did last night. The party was magnificent, and it was good to see everyone, even if it wasn't as relaxed a debut for the quads as we had hoped that it would be."

"The formal holiday portraits turned out wonderfully, by the way! I just got the proofs. I'll email them to you, too."

"Thanks." They talked a little more, then hung up.

Chase turned the heat up under the skillet. "So it's all good with your mother?"

The smell of sizzling bacon wafted through the room. Mitzy put four slices of bread in the toaster. "Better than I would have thought."

Chase broke four eggs into a second skillet, sunny-side up. "She's mellowed."

Because of the unconditional love she shares with Walter. Mitzy smiled. "I suppose we all have."

He wrapped an arm about her shoulder and brought her close. Mitzy's heart raced at the warm, intimate contact. She splayed her hands over the hardness of his chest and looked up at him, wondering how she had ever managed to be happy without him. "Have I thanked you for all your help lately?" she asked softly.

A wicked gleam filled his eyes, and then he bent to kiss her temple. "Numerous times, in numerous ways, last night."

He drew back to meet her gaze and she blushed at the erotically charged memories. She shook her head, smiling playfully. "You wouldn't have thought we'd have the energy."

Looking every bit as happy and content as she felt, he brushed the pad of his thumb across the curve of her lips. "That's what happens when you're making up for lost time," he teased, lowering his head. His hands clamped over her shoulders as their lips met. The kiss was hot and slow and every bit as electrifying as their lovemaking had been. Yet she could feel his hesitation. Like there was something else…something more important…he wanted from her.

With a sigh, they drew apart. His expression tender— and inscrutable—Chase wrapped his hands around her waist and asked, "Did you really mean to invite me to join you-all for Christmas?"

Ah, so that was it. Mitzy searched her heart and found the answer. "Yes, I did," she admitted sincerely. She lifted her hand. "But I also don't want you to feel pressured." The way they both had pressured each other when they were engaged. "I know you have your own family gatherings, too."

Flashing a relaxed smile, he reached out and tucked an errant strand of her hair behind her ear. "I do, but it's nothing that your entire family couldn't tag along and enjoy, too. Especially the lavish dinner at my folks' ranch on Christmas night."

"Rachel and Frank wouldn't mind you showing up with

eight extra guests?" When they already had six kids, two daughters-in-law, and seven grandchildren? And heaven knew who else?

"Are you kidding?" Chase beamed. "They'd love it. And so would I."

At her prodding, Chase checked to be sure, and by evening, Mitzy and family had a formal invitation from Chase's parents. Mitzy talked to Judith and Walter and everyone RSVP'd yes.

And Chase still hadn't left.

Partly because she hadn't expected to be back from Dallas until late, and hence had no volunteer help coming. And partly because they were enjoying being together, all six of them, so very much.

This, Mitzy thought contentedly as the day drew to a close and nighttime beckoned, was what being part of a traditional family unit would feel like. Satisfying. Poignant. And wonderful.

So wonderful she was beginning to regret ever asking Chase for "closure" to their original relationship.

But maybe that, too, like their breakup, could eventually be undone.

Aware it was turning out to be a very happy holiday season after all, she faced off with him next to the Christmas tree. "So what do you think?" she asked mischievously. "*Are* you up to the demanding task of helping with baths?" He certainly looked capable of anything. Including and especially making love to her again.

"Of course I am," he said with cocky assurance, flexing the muscles in his shoulders and chest. He paused to chuckle. "Only one problem. I've never actually *bathed* an infant. Never mind four at one time."

If he could diaper and feed them, he could do this, too. "Not to worry. I've got a system down pat, and I'll teach it to you, too." Mitzy demonstrated as she talked, and Chase followed her lead. "The first thing I do is undress all four babies and wrap them in their hooded bath towels to stay warm. Then place them in their stroller, like so." She undressed Joe and Zach. Chase disrobed Alex and Gabe.

With all four comfortably settled, Chase wheeled the stroller into the kitchen. He and all four boys watched with interest as she set up a bathing station with the baby bathtub on the counter, next to the sink, filled the bottom of the tub with warm water, laid out the liquid baby soap and washcloths and a cup for rinsing.

"Who's going to go first?" Chase queried, moving the stroller gently back and forth in a rocking motion.

"Joe." Mitzy gently unwrapped her infant son. Guided him down into the semisitting-up position in the water. Chase stepped in to take her place, while she quickly but gently got Joe sudsed up, rinsed and out.

Chase held the towel, and she placed Joe into his arms, wrapping him up to stay warm. He went back in his stroller seat.

And so it went. Mitzy and Chase worked in tandem, bathing Zach, Alex and Gabe. Finished, they wheeled the four baby boys back into the family room, where their bassinets awaited. One by one, they were cuddled, diapered and dressed.

Bottles warmed, Mitzy and Chase sat down side by side on the sofa, double nursing pillows on their laps, and fed them.

As the boys hungrily took their bottles, Chase shook his head in wonderment. "I can't believe we did all that in what…?"

Mitzy grinned, pleased it had gone so well, too. "Half an hour," she said. "When I first brought them home from the hospital it used to take an hour and a half to do all that, and that was when I had three helpers."

"Practice makes perfect?"

"Something like that."

Contentment permeated the room. The quads looked up at both of them adoringly as they nestled comfortably on Mitzy's and Chase's laps and drank from their bottles.

The moment was so perfect, in fact, it didn't seem quite real. Making Mitzy wonder what would happen when the newness of all this faded, along with the undeniable magic of the holiday season, and reality sank in for her and Chase. Would he still want to spend so much time with them? Or would it be back to business as usual, with his boundless professional ambition once again taking the lead...

She couldn't imagine how devastated she would feel if that were the case. Especially since everything was so fairy-tale perfect right now. Chase turned to look at her, his broad shoulder nudging hers. Apparently, he was feeling the joy, too. "You're amazing, you know that?" he murmured tenderly.

She shook her head modestly. "I've kind of had to be." There simply had been no other choice. "But I didn't always feel I could handle this. When I first found out I was having four babies..."

He put Alex on his shoulder to burp. "You didn't expect it?"

Mitzy did the same with Joe. "I went in for artificial insemination when I was ovulating. It was the first attempt, so they tried to prepare me for the possibility that it wouldn't 'take.' But it did. And there I was. A single mom, with four babies coming, instead of the one I had planned on."

Chase grinned as Alex let out a loud belch. "How did Judith and Walter react?"

Mitzy continued patting Joe gently on the back. She looked over at Chase, marveling at how quickly he was becoming adept at all this. Candidly, she admitted, "They had all the emotions I had. Joy. Disbelief. Fear, because it was going to be a difficult gestation, as most multiple pregnancies are."

Chase stroked the back of his hand over Mitzy's cheek. "But you-all made it," he observed softly.

Briefly, Mitzy leaned into his adoring touch. "We did. Although I have to confess that more than once I wished..." She stopped short, aware the intimacy of the situation was prompting her to reveal way too much.

With a shake of her head, she turned her attention to her four babies and said nothing more.

Chase was silent, too, focusing on the last of the feeding ritual. Finally, all four had finished their bottles and were put back in their bassinets.

Feeling way too emotional, Mitzy picked up the damp baby towels and discarded clothing and disposable diapers, and made her way toward the laundry room. As before, Chase was right beside her, helping.

Ready to pick up where they'd left off.

He hooked his hands over her shoulders. "What do you wish, Mitzy?"

Gazing up at him, she sighed. Where had holding back ever gotten her?

She needed to unburden herself to him.

Her spine to the washing machine, hands braced on either side of her, Mitzy searched within her heart and somehow found the courage to admit with unprecedented honesty, "That I wasn't going through this alone." She shook her head, jerked in a breath. "That I had—" Her voice caught. Once again, she was unable to go on.

He moved in so they were touching in one electrified

line. Cupping her face in his big, strong hands, he tilted her face up to his so she had no choice but to look into his eyes as he finished softly for her, "A husband?"

Self-conscious heat filled her face. "I don't want to get married just to have a partner to go through life with or help raise my sons."

"Understandable," he said quietly. "I feel the same way." He paused, wanting to delve deeper yet. "But surely there's someone…"

Was he fishing for compliments? Trying to figure out where they stood? It seemed so. Once again, she called on herself to be brave. She looked him in the eye. "You have always been the only man I could ever imagine myself marrying."

He regarded her with steadfast care. "Same here." His voice deepened and he continued in a calm, deliberate voice, "If you weren't going to be my wife, I didn't know who possibly could be. It's why I never got engaged again."

"Why I didn't, either," Mitzy confessed, her pulse racing at the new heat in his eyes.

Chase lifted her onto the washer and stepped between her knees. "So," he said heavily, resting the flat of his palms on her upper thighs. "What are we going to do about this?"

"Besides make love?"

"Besides make love."

A palpable silence fell.

"I don't know," she admitted, feeling the barriers around her heart fall, one by one. Going through the box of memorabilia the night before had left her feeling sentimental all day. Spending so much time with Chase, and the babies, traveling with him, taking him home again, had only amplified that. "What do you want to do?"

She splayed her hands on the warm, hard contours of

his chest and searched his eyes. She wondered if he was feeling the same soul-deep need and yearning she was. She definitely saw an undeniable affection that seemed to have only grown stronger during their time apart. And something that hadn't necessarily been there before, a need to hear whatever she had to say.

Mitzy swallowed around the new ache in her throat. "I meant what I said the other day about not wanting another long engagement." If she got as serious about Chase as she felt she was about to be.

"I meant it, too," he said gruffly. "It's either going to be right, or it's not."

"And if it is," Mitzy continued, agreeing, "I'd rather simply go for it and elope than have it turn into the kind of bridal extravaganza in Dallas that my mother is going to want."

"You could always do a small ceremony first, a large party or reception later."

Were they planning their wedding? The one they wanted. Plus the way to make their families happy...

It seemed so.

And yet...

Seeming to realize he was rushing her again, that *they* were rushing things, he paused, proceeding carefully now. "I want to be part of your life, Mitzy." His gaze stroked her features, each one, ending with her eyes. "Part of the boys' life. They're going to need a father—" he paused again, then continued awkwardly "—er...figure."

It was unlike him to stumble over his words. Yet she understood his caution. They were moving so fast. *Too* fast?

"What about you, Chase?" she asked, deciding maybe it was time for her to put the spotlight on him. "What do you need?"

His sensual smile widened and his eyes shuttered to

half-mast. "You…" He pulled her against him. Desire floated through her, whisper soft. Still kissing her, he shifted her all the way to the edge of the machine, lifted her legs and wrapped them about his waist. She tugged off his sweater and T-shirt. He whisked off her sweater and bra. They came together, the sensitive tips of her breasts brushing the taut sinew of his chest. And then they kissed again, letting their feelings sweep them into passion.

For too long she had let herself believe she could be happy alone, that she could have children on her own and never need anything else.

However, Chase's reappearance in her life had shown her otherwise. He'd let her see there was so much more to life to enjoy. If only she had the courage to pursue it.

And that wasn't hard to find when he deepened their kiss until it was so wild and reckless it stole her breath. Unable to turn away from the sweet, aching need flowing between them, she surged against him, savoring the safety and comfort of being cradled in his strong arms. Lower still, his hardness elicited a wellspring of tingles. Her fingers fell to the waistband of his jeans, and then his mouth was on her flesh, creating an even hotter frenzy of wanting.

The rest of their clothes fell to the floor. Sheathing himself, he brought her against him, taking possession of her with earth-shattering skill and affection. She opened to meet him, savoring his heat and his hardness. And still they kissed, their mouths mating as avidly as their bodies. Until there was no more holding back, no more pretending they didn't need and want each other as much as they needed and wanted this. Together, they went soaring into bliss, and slowly, incredibly, wonderfully came back down.

They took the babies upstairs and tucked them into their cribs, then made love again in her bed. Afterward, Chase held Mitzy against him. He was happier than he had been in a long time. Yet frustrated, too, because he knew he was still a long way from getting her to take that final leap of faith and say yes to marrying him.

Loving the feel of her head on his chest and her soft body pressed up against his, he stroked a hand through her hair. Hating for anything to spoil the magic of the moment, yet sensing something was bothering her, he finally prodded gently, "Something on your mind, sweetheart?"

Mitzy sighed and lifted her head, looking relieved to finally admit, "I'm always telling the people I've counseled in the course of my social work not to rush things. That if *it's right*, an emotional connection *will stand* the test of time."

Chase thought of everyone he knew with a solid marriage and happy family life. "That's true. It will." *Ours definitely has...*

She nodded. Resting her chin on her fist, she continued, while looking deeply into his eyes, "But, on the other hand, I also know that too much caution, too much holding back, can be equally dangerous." She sat up, dragging the sheet over the soft curves of her breasts. "Because sometimes if you slow things down too much life gets in the way again and you don't get that second chance," she worried aloud.

"Life" as in her family business troubles?

Or something else?

Something more…?

He joined her, sitting against the headboard. Reaching over, he took her hand in his. "I guess the trick is finding that middle ground," Chase replied carefully. He lifted the inside of her wrist to his lips.

"Not moving too fast. Not keeping the barriers up around your heart."

Which, as it happened, was exactly what he and Mitzy were trying to do, Chase thought.

Find that middle ground and stick to it.

Mitzy shifted toward him, the sheet dropping low across her breasts. "The funny thing is, Chase," she said as her bent knee pressed against his thigh, "playing it safe is suddenly not what I feel like I'm doing *at all*." And they both knew that wasn't typical.

"Me, either," Chase confessed, his lower body hardening. Even though he knew in most cases slow and steady won the race.

Appearing to fear that it was all going to blow up in their faces, she raked her teeth across her kiss-swollen lower lip. "Think it's the holidays making us so wildly impatient and reckless?" she asked, squinting at him hopefully.

Or love, Chase thought.

Found.

And squandered.

And now found again.

But sensing she wasn't ready to hear anything that serious or binding, at least not tonight, he merely eased her back down onto the pillows, glided a hand down her midriff, lower still. Then smiled and rumbled, "I think—" he kissed her throat, her collarbone, the taut tip of one breast "—this is the time of year when wishes come true."

She shuddered with pleasure. "Oh, cowboy..."

"Oh" was right.

He rolled, so she was beneath him, caught her wrists in both hands, secured them on either side of her head and captured her lips with his. As she arched against him, he kissed her sweetly, hotly, deeply.

Plundering, until she kissed him back. Again and again and again.

"And speaking of what I wish for…" he said, working his way down her body. Past her navel to the sweet, silky wetness.

She arched against him and let out a sultry chuckle. "Round three?"

Savoring the increasing intimacy between them, he spread her legs and whispered back, "Sweetheart, you read my mind."

Chapter Thirteen

Chase was long gone by the time Mitzy's helpers arrived early Monday morning. Bess Monroe, who was known to be grinchy around the holidays, studied Mitzy as she took off her coat and hung it up. Finally noting with delight, "You look really happy. I know you have a lot to celebrate this year, with the quads and all…"

Her twin sister, Bridgett Monroe McCabe, wife to Chase's brother Cullen, winked. "I think it's all that, plus the love of her life."

Mitzy tilted her head, pretending to be perplexed. "And who would that be exactly?"

Bess chuckled. "Your former fiancé. The ruggedly handsome Chase McCabe, of course."

Chase was making her happy, Mitzy admitted. So much so that she didn't quite trust it. She didn't want to go through her days waiting for the next seemingly in-surmountable problem. The way she had before, when his ambition had constantly come between them. And she hadn't really tried to understand where he was coming from. Never mind support his life goals or cut him any slack. Now, years later, she could see her dad had been right about Chase. He had always been destined for greater things...

"Speaking of Chase," Bridgett said, pausing to see the memorabilia Mitzy had spread out over the kitchen island.

Too late, Mitzy realized she should have kept everything in the box until she was alone. "I was making up an album."

Bess lifted a brow. "Looks like it goes pretty far back."

"And includes the formal announcement of your engagement," Bridgett noted.

Bess, who was normally as cautious as Mitzy, looked taken aback. "The program for your wedding ceremony—if it had happened."

Mitzy recalled how upset and disappointed Judith had been that it hadn't. "Are the two of you getting back together?" Bridgett persisted.

Mitzy lifted a hand, wordlessly pleading the Fifth. "I don't know. I got this stuff out the other day, and I thought I should probably organize it, instead of just leaving it stuffed in a box." She looked at the twins sternly. "And I would really appreciate it if you *didn't* tell Chase."

Identical grins flashed. "Is it a surprise for him?" Bridgett asked hopefully.

"A little one," Mitzy conceded. Or big, if he took the gesture the way she privately hoped he would... She shrugged. "You know how sentimental people can be around the holidays."

The twins watched Mitzy hastily gather things up and put them away. "So we repeat, are you and Chase getting back together officially?"

Were they?

It seemed so.

But then, she'd thought she would marry him, too.

And that hadn't happened.

"All I can tell you is that we're taking it one day at a time."
She found her bag and keys. "And speaking of today, I don't
know how long it's going to take me to do the business meeting on my schedule, so I've got more help to relieve you-all
at two p.m., if need be, and I've written out instructions for
even longer than that, just in case…" *Things are even worse
at MCS than I already suspect,* she finished silently.

Her friends wished her luck, and Mitzy was out the
door.

Unfortunately, the meeting at the CPA was as bad as
she had feared it would be. Having realized just how much
help she was going to need to turn things around at MCS,
she headed straight out to Chase's ranch, where he said
he'd be if she wanted to talk to him about the results of
the internal audit.

To her surprise, she wasn't his only visitor at the Knotty
Pine.

MCS's COO Buck Phillips's dark green pickup truck
was parked in front of Chase's ranch house. The two men
were standing on the porch, deep in what looked like a
surprisingly friendly but sober discussion as Mitzy drove
up and parked.

The two men shook hands.

Feeling shut out and betrayed, Mitzy emerged from
her SUV.

Wondering if her life was about to implode all over
again, she spoke to Buck first. "I'm surprised to see you
all the way out here." *Especially since you've been telling
me not to trust Chase! And were the one who encouraged*

me to get the audit from the CPA firm, rather than just let Chase do it.

Buck ignored her upset. "Chase and I had business to discuss."

"Martin Custom Saddle company business?" Mitzy probed.

The men exchanged glances. Chase nodded slightly. Buck turned back to Mitzy. "I know about your father's request to Chase and what Chase promised him in return, too. Gus told me before he passed."

So blindsided that she stumbled as she mounted the steps, Mitzy gaped. "Is there anyone besides me who *didn't* know?"

Chase caught her around the waist and helped her the rest of the way onto the porch. His grip as protective as ever. When he was sure she was steady, he let her go and stepped back. "Gus just talked to Buck, Judith and Walter, and me, Mitzy."

Her indignation grew. "Well, that makes me feel better," she huffed, the heat of Chase's touch still making her tingle.

She whirled back to Buck. "So if you knew my dad wanted Chase involved," she started emotionally, "why did you tell me not to trust Chase?"

"Because I didn't think I could count on him to do the right thing."

Buck picked up on the awareness simmering between her and Chase. His craggy features softened. "But I was wrong about Chase, Mitzy," he said quietly. "I should have been encouraging you to listen to his advice all along, instead of letting my own emotions…about what Chase tried to do, years ago…blind me. You need to listen to him, too."

Buck shook hands with Chase. "Let me know if you need anything else regarding the financials," he said, man-to-man. To Mitzy, Buck tipped his hat, then settled it square on his head. "I'll see you at the MCS holiday party on Saturday, if not before." He headed off to his truck.

Tension simmered between Mitzy and Chase.

Seeming to understand he had made a big mistake in not telling her in advance of his meeting with Buck, Chase said, "Let's go inside and discuss this."

Mitzy was not in the mood to be placated. She folded her arms in front of her and forced a mirthless smile. "Let's not."

Chase regarded her steadily, no more willing to give up on this than he was on the two of them. "I can bring all the data out here that I just showed Buck," he offered cordially, coming close enough to inundate her with his crisp leather-and-pine scent. "Or you can go inside and view it there." He paused to let his words sink in. "It's up to you."

He had a point. She was being childish. Hadn't she come over here to get his help and his advice? "Fine." She brushed past him and strode into the wing that housed his business. A lot of which seemed to be conducted at home.

Mitzy stared in mute amazement.

There were huge placards on easels showcasing new marketing plans built around her dad's legendary image. Financial data, much of it in red, showing the current miserable state of the business. Projections on what could be.

She exhaled roughly. "I'm guessing you already know what the CPA firm just told me—that my dad's company is on the brink of bankruptcy."

Chase nodded, appearing neither surprised nor alarmed. He took her hand. "Buck just gave me the details."

"And...?" Mitzy resisted the urge to break down in tears.

He squeezed her fingers gently and led her over to sit down. "You need a million in cash to pay off the existing debt, give out holiday bonuses and make the kind of capital investment needed to get MCS not just back on sound fiscal footing but at the top of its game."

He may as well have been talking about a billion dollars. It was so far out of her league. With a deflated sigh, she settled in the oversize leather reading chair. "I don't have that," she said glumly. "I don't even have the money for the bonuses."

Once again he did not look surprised. Or, she noted curiously, even particularly dismayed. "Do *you* have that kind of cash just sitting around?" she asked, incredulous.

Chase shook his head, once again the levelheaded businessman, driven to the core. He settled on the ottoman in front of her, so they were face-to-face and knee to knee. "No," he said, all signs of the tenderhearted lover she adored fading. He paused to look her in the eye, even more serious now. "But I can get it *if* I do what your father asked of me and buy the company by year's end."

Buy MCS? When he knew she was opposed to selling out? To anyone?

His dispassionate attitude made her angry and scared. This was obviously all just another deal to him, an asset to add to his leather goods empire. To her, it was the culmination of everything her father had spent his entire life building.

She knew what her father had apparently told others he wanted. For her to be relieved of the enormous stress of running his company. But she still wasn't sure ending her family's connection to the company was the right thing.

Especially since she hadn't really yet tried to effectively run MCS. Feeling disgruntled and upset, Mitzy searched for another option.

Maybe they needed to stop thinking about long-term plans. And concentrate on the immediate needs.

She rose stiffly and stepped to the side, to put a more suitable distance between them. "How about the two hundred thousand dollars I need for Christmas bonuses?" She moved behind the chair, curving her hands over the back of it. "Do you have that?"

Shaking his head, Chase stood, too. "Not without first purchasing the company. It's not just me at McCabe Leather Goods, Mitzy. It hasn't been for a long time. I answer to a board of directors and am required to demonstrate appropriate fiscal judgment in every action I take."

She focused on the downward curve of his sensual lips. "Or…?" What were his risks? She knew hers…

His eyes narrowed even more. "If they perceive me as being reckless, or not exercising sound business acumen, the board could vote me out as CEO. I'd still have a fifty-one percent share of McCabe Leather Goods, but I would no longer be in control of everything that went on there, the way I am now."

"And you're not about to risk that."

"No." He continued to study her as if trying to figure something out. His expression turned as implacable as his voice. "I'm not."

Feeling abruptly transported back to a much unhappier time in her life, when it had always been business—and ambition—first, Mitzy rushed past him. "I have to get out of here."

He caught her arm, stopping her forward motion, and swung her around to face him. The reserve was back in his stormy blue eyes, along with lingering desire. "Mitzy, please. Sit down and calm down." He brought her closer still, wrapping both arms around her waist. "Let's talk about this, and go through all the options logically."

She splayed her hands across his chest and worked to keep the disillusionment out of her voice. "Logically?"

Emotion welled within her. "My father's legacy is at risk, Chase!"

He continued to hold her stubbornly. The chivalrous, protective look was back in his eyes. "Exactly my point," he countered with gruff affection.

She knew how convincing Chase could be. She also knew this was something she needed to handle on her own. Because if she didn't at least try to figure out how to hang on a little while longer, she would always wonder if she'd given up too easily.

She extricated herself from his arms. Ignoring his entreating look, she shook her head at him. "I have to think…" *Have to find another way…* Heart pounding, she rushed out.

By the time she got back home, she knew what she had to do. She said hello to the new shift of volunteers and checked on the boys, then went into her father's old study. The fact it had never been redone had once been comforting to her. Now, as she sat behind his massive wooden desk, she felt even more disloyal. As if she'd let him down. Worse, it seemed Gus had known in advance she would do so, just hadn't had the heart to tell her.

Determined to do a better job of protecting the MCS employees than she had done thus far, she picked up her cell phone and asked to FaceTime with her stepfather.

Maybe because she never called him, especially during the workday, Walter picked up immediately. He was wearing a suit and tie, and was obviously in some kind of business meeting at his Dallas office.

He stepped all the way out of the boardroom, shutting the door behind him. "Mitzy, darling, what is it? What's wrong?"

She told him. "If you could just loan me the money for the bonuses, Walter, so I can hand them out at Christmas—"

and not have to sell out to Chase "—I promise I'll pay you back every penny."

Walter, who was usually quick to indulge her even when she didn't want to be indulged, frowned. "If I did that, your mother would never forgive me," he replied kindly but firmly.

Stunned, Mitzy sputtered, "But..."

Walter moved down the hall and into his private office, again shutting the door behind him, insuring them total privacy. "She's my wife. My first responsibility is to her."

"I'll talk to Mother..." Mitzy promised desperately.

Walter sat down behind his desk with a sigh. "Please don't. A conversation like that will only make you both unhappy. You know how she feels about the business."

It was Mitzy's turn to sigh unhappily. She parroted back, "That my father's devotion to MCS caused the demise of their marriage."

Walter nodded, looking just as concerned. "And right now, rightly or wrongly, she feels the very same thing is happening to you."

Walter's last words before they hung up ten minutes later—*Chase is there to help you, Mitzy, let him*—resonated with Mitzy throughout the rest of the afternoon.

She thought about texting him and telling him not to come by for the 8:00 p.m.-to-midnight shift, but couldn't quite make herself do it.

The part of her that had been hurt before by him, the part that had played second fiddle to his business goals and ambitions, had to see if the same thing held true now.

So she bathed her boys early. One at a time. And somehow managed to use her system to do it all by herself. Without a tear being shed in the process.

Well, if you could discount the ones welling up inside her, that was.

Finished, she was just about to feed her four boys when the doorbell rang.

Chase stood on the doorstep. A cold front was blowing in. He looked as sexy as ever, with his cheeks ruddy from the cold winter weather, his hair windblown, his smoky-blue eyes intent. His cashmere sweater and dark jeans hugged the masculine lines of his body, and the collar of his suede jacket was turned up against his throat. The multicolored Christmas lights he'd helped string across her porch framed him spectacularly, evoking the wonder of the season.

Without warning, a rush of optimism flowed through her. Yes, she had huge problems but this was also the season for miracles.

As Chase caught sight of her, pleasure lit his handsome features. "I hope this isn't the part where you shoo away the messenger," he quipped.

Was she glad or unhappy to see him?

Mostly, Mitzy decided, she was feeling relieved.

Because he hadn't quite given up on them.

Just as she hadn't quite given up, either.

"Of course not," she joshed back. "My manners are better than that." She chuckled. "Usually, anyway." Chase did have a way of getting under her skin like no one else ever had, or, she suspected, ever would. She stepped back to usher him inside.

Chase is there to help you, Walter had said. *Let him...*

He shrugged out of his jacket and hung it up. "How are the little dudes this evening?" he asked amiably.

"Ready for their eight p.m. bottles. Or at least they will be when they wake up. They drifted off again, after their baths."

"Can I help?"

Mitzy walked over to the bassinets. All four had their eyes shut, but there was a little shifting here and there. Which meant they'd be awake soon.

She led the way into the kitchen and slid the bottles into the warmers to heat. "I'm sure they'd love that."

Chase caught her hand and turned her to face him. "What about you?" he rasped as she collided with the hard sinew of his tall body. His eyes darkened mysteriously. "Would you love that?"

Emotion welled. The uncertainty from years before came back to plague her. She swallowed, cautioning, "Chase..."

"I know this is difficult for you, Mitzy. Your dad knew it would be. Buck Phillips, the rest of the employees, know it, too."

Tears blurred her eyes. "I feel like I'm letting everyone down."

"You're not," he assured gruffly.

She wished she could believe that. And yet...

Silence fell.

Chase tucked his hand beneath her chin and lifted her gaze to his. Sober, yet encouraging, too. "Will you trust me to do as your father asked, in the way that he asked me to do so?" His low gravelly voice sent a thrill down her spine. "That ensures his company and legacy go on as proudly as it always has, the MCS employees' interests protected, too?"

Mitzy forced herself to momentarily put aside her fear of failure and do as everyone else had advised. "All right," she said finally. "If you put together an offer, I'll seriously consider it."

"That's all I'm asking." He smiled with brisk assurance.

But was it?

Mitzy wondered.

* * *

To Mitzy's disappointment, Chase was gone the rest of the week. She understood he had to be in Dallas–Fort Worth to put together the deal with the bank and his board of directors.

They spoke every night on the phone.

She still missed him.

More than when they'd ended their engagement.

And that scared her, too.

What had she done in opening herself up to this kind of pain again? And so quickly?

Had she been someone she was counseling as a social worker, Mitzy would have read herself the riot act.

She was still grieving the loss of her father, and therefore very vulnerable.

She had four infants to focus on.

A steady, secure life she'd spent a decade building.

And now, on a romantic whim and the unexpected, unusual need to be suddenly rescued, she was considering all sorts of things that would have been unthinkable less than a month before.

All those were big trouble signs.

Countered by the feelings Chase always engendered inside her.

The truth was, she wanted this to work out.

She needed them to find a way to be together, as they hadn't before. And most of all she yearned for a complete family for her sons, the kind she had given up on when she signed up to have the babies on her own, via AI.

Chase had changed that.

He had shown her what it would be like to have a man by her side as she brought up her children.

She wanted that, more than was comfortable to admit.

So, while he was gone, she busied herself by alter-

nately taking care of the quads and baking cookies for
the MCS party. She even spent some time working on
Chase's Christmas gift—the memorabilia album that she
had lovingly assembled, chronicling their early years together to the present.

It was sweet and sentimental. Just the way she hoped
their future would one day be.

Chase sat at the table in his downtown loft, going over
the deal with his mother, who had come to Fort Worth to
do some holiday shopping. And, per his urgent request,
stopped in to meet with him.

"Just give me the bottom line," he urged, figuring if
anyone could find another way, it would be his brilliant
tax-and-business attorney parent.

Rachel sighed and sat back in her chair. "As you can
see, the date of the sale is going to make a huge difference in the financials." She paused to point out several
different sets of numbers. "You don't have a choice, and
neither does the board, if you want to maximize capital
and turn the business around." She peered at him. "Surely,
your own team of lawyers and accountants have already
told you this."

Chase rubbed at the tense muscles at the back of his
neck. "They have."

Rachel lifted a brow. "Then…?"

Chase shrugged. "I was just hoping for a different option." The kind of miracle that would put both him and
Mitzy on the same page.

Rachel took another sip of hot chamomile tea, guessed,
"You don't think Mitzy is going to like the required time-
line."

Tension knotted Chase's gut. Which was unusual. Usually, he did not allow himself to get emotional about a business deal. "I know she won't."

"Given a little time, she'll understand."

Would she? Chase tried to picture that but couldn't quite make it happen. He stood and went over to the sink to pour his own tepid black coffee down the sink. He forced himself to be as pragmatic as the situation required. "She may eventually be relieved to not worry about running the business, even from afar, though."

"Even happy about it," Rachel predicted.

That was a stretch. Chase shook his head. He looked at the Christmas photo of Mitzy and the quads he had taken on her bed. She had made it into a Christmas postcard for her friends. And given him a couple of the extras. One was tucked in a clear pocket in his briefcase, the other on the fridge at his ranch house.

He turned back to his mom, aware she was still waiting for his assessment. "I don't think she's going to be anywhere near ecstatic." Even though he had made sure that she and her children would benefit financially, too.

Rachel's brow furrowed. "Why not?"

Because he knew there was one aspect of the deal not in the financials his mother had just reviewed that Mitzy was going to find very hard to take. Especially when she already felt crushed and humiliated by her own naïveté and MCS's near bankruptcy.

Rachel waited.

With a reluctant grimace, Chase explained, "She's going to be upset because she thinks she always knows what's best, and most of the time she does…"

"Just not in the business world," his mother interjected quietly, getting up to reheat her tea.

Chase moved aside. "It's not her thing. Any more than it really was Gus's." He watched his mother punch the beverage button on the microwave. "I mean, both are... were...incredibly talented, intuitive people, but when it comes to making the hard decisions that business sometimes required..."

"She can't do it."

Chase felt another punch in the gut. "Not so far."

His mother removed her mug. "Probably not ever?"

Reluctantly, Chase forced himself to admit this was so.

Another silence fell. Rachel studied him over the rim, putting two and two together. "You think she will blame *you* for having to do it?"

He forced himself to be as optimistic as he always was when a long-held goal was within reach. Yes, there would be a few difficult moments. Incredibly difficult moments. But they would get past them. He had taken steps to see to that.

Figuring he could use his mother's advice on this, too, he went to get the Christmas gift he had prepared for Mitzy. One that would allow her the kind of choice she would not have in the business deal.

"I'm hoping, when Mitzy has time to think about it, that she will see the MCS transaction as the beginning to the future we always should have had. And to that end..." He brought the present he was planning to give to Mitzy to the kitchen island.

As Rachel studied the two sets of plans and saw what he was proposing, she put her hand over her heart. "Oh, Chase..." She looked as overcome as he felt in that moment.

And then cautiously reserved.

Once again, in his eagerness to get ahead, he felt he might have made a mistake. He continued reading his mom's expression. Sighed. "Too much?"

Rachel regarded him with the no-holds-barred maternal honesty for which she was known. "Given what else you're about to do…what I imagine you have to do… I think you're walking a tightrope with absolutely no safety net beneath you."

Chase swallowed, aware that once again he had been put in an impossible situation. Forced to choose between what he knew in his heart was the only way to save a company otherwise doomed for failure, and the most important person in his life. "She still cares for me, Mom." *Still wants a life with me, as much as I want one with her.* "I can feel it."

Rachel gently patted his arm. "I saw that, too, the day we were all together cutting down our Christmas trees at your ranch."

But was that devotion going to be enough?

Chase had to hope it was.

Chapter Fourteen

"I don't understand," Mitzy said, meeting Chase outside the large Victorian on Spring Street that—because of its neglect—had been on the market for the last six months, nary a buyer in sight.

She peered at him in confusion. "Why did you send Lulu and Bess over to babysit and ask me to meet you here this morning? When you and I haven't seen each other since Tuesday." A fact that hurt her immensely, even though she knew he had been busy working on a solution for her family business.

With a beleaguered sigh, she finished indignantly, "And we have the holiday party at MCS this afternoon!"

"I know you have a lot on your agenda this morning, darlin'." Chase slid his hand beneath her elbow and led her up the walk. Inside the empty home, all the lights were on. "We still need to talk business, too."

She blinked as he escorted her across the threshold. "Regarding MCS?"

His gaze steady, he shut the door behind them. "Yes."

All she knew thus far was that he had managed to secure the holiday bonuses for her employees, to be given out this afternoon at the conclusion of the party, as per usual.

He led her through the formal rooms at the front of the home. "But I really wanted to show you this first."

He hadn't dropped his hold on her and her body warmed beneath his touch. "Why?"

"Because I'm thinking of buying and renovating it."

Her midriff fluttering, she stepped back. "What about the Knotty Pine?"

He lifted one broad shoulder in a careless shrug. "I haven't decided yet. I may keep it as an investment. And rent it out. Or use it as a weekend retreat. Sort of depends on how you feel."

How *she* felt? Since when did he ask her advice on anything? Never mind something this important!

Expression serious, he led her through a hall lined with hideous purple wallpaper toward the kitchen. Blueprints were stretched over every ancient countertop. He led her to the first set of plans. "This is what could be done with the home you inherited from your dad, if you want to stay there as the boys grow. But the backyard is kind of small already, so if you expand, it'll be cut back to near nothing. Which could be a problem with four active children."

"Okay."

He guided her to the next set of renovation plans. "Over here, we have plans for this house. It's got seven bedrooms and three baths upstairs. A half bath and five rooms downstairs that could be configured however you like—but the architect suggested we do two studies, a dedicated playroom and then make the rest into one large kitchen-dining-family area."

He led her to the bay window overlooking the backyard, which was overrun with weeds and a set of extremely overgrown magnolia bushes that served as a fence. "It would need new landscaping, of course. But, as you can see, there's also room for a garden and a nice play area for the boys out back."

"Mmm-hmm." She still had no idea what he was getting at.

He turned back to her, hands lifted expansively. Grinned. "Merry Christmas! Depending on what you choose, I can do either, or both if you're not ready for us to move in together yet."

Mitzy blinked. Chase had a reputation for moving full steam ahead when he really wanted something. But even for someone as blatantly ambitious as he was, this was way too much. "You're asking us to cohabit," she ascertained slowly, her emotions in turmoil.

His eyes narrowed. "I think it would be better for the boys, since we live in Laramie, if we got married or at the very least engaged, but again, that's up to you." He studied her patiently. "I'll do whatever you want."

What if I want you to love me? she thought wistfully. *What if I want you to stop acting so scary resolute, as if everything is already decided?* When, in truth, because of all that was left unresolved, nothing was.

She took his hand, and feeling the need for some air, led him through the rickety screen door to the wraparound porch overlooking the backyard.

Glad she had yet to put on her party clothes and was still in jeans, boots and a zip-up fleece, she guided him to an old glider with a faded vinyl cushion seat. She sat down and patted the place beside her.

He took a seat, too.

She took his hand, aware she had seen this kind of panic often in her line of work. It usually happened when a person's entire life was about to blow up, and they knew it, even if they couldn't admit it.

"Before we decide any of that…" Although she already knew what she was going to say to his incredibly misguided proposal—no!—she counseled, "We need to back up. Let's start with the easiest thing. The business. Did the McCabe Leather Goods board of directors agree to fund the revitalization and purchase of Martin Custom Saddle before the end of the year, so MCS's future will be secure?"

"Yes. As I told you, they also agreed to pay out the end-of-year bonuses. I have the bank checks in my briefcase. As well as the purchase papers you will need to sign before I can give those out."

Mitzy laid a hand across her heart. "Well, that's a relief." The MCS employees would have a merry Christmas, after all.

He tightened his hand on hers, stood. "There were a few more stipulations, though."

Her pulse escalating once again, she waited.

"They want new leadership and I agree with them. To turn the company around, we will need to bring in someone to swiftly implement all the changes and run the business."

She didn't like his brisk, all-business tone. "You're replacing Buck Phillips?"

"Putting him in another role, one he is more suited for."

Suddenly needing her space, she stood and moved a short distance away. She spun back to face Chase. "Will there be a reduction in his salary?"

"No." Chase stood, too. He moved toward her amiably. "Everyone is going to make the same salary as they were making before, with a possibility of a raise when we successfully turn the business around."

Relief rushed through her. "Okay."

"We're firing you."

She took in his impassive expression. Surely, she couldn't have heard right. "What did you just say?"

"The board of directors is mandating a new CEO from outside the company be put in place to run the revitalization, so we're firing you."

"We," she repeated numbly. So Chase included himself in this decision?

Chase nodded. "It's common practice in situations like this."

Was that supposed to be reassuring?

"We already have someone in mind. She already works for my company, and has experience bringing other failing small businesses into our brand and turning them around."

"Let me get this straight," she repeated, a mixture of shock and anger roiling in her gut. "You are *personally* firing me?"

She saw a brief flicker of regret, followed by his inherent pragmatism. "I told the board I wanted to do it. I thought it would go down better this way."

Mitzy didn't know whether to laugh or cry. In truth, she felt like doing a little of both.

The closeness they'd built faded. Replaced by the withering animosity that had been the hallmark of their previous breakup.

She glared at him, not understanding how he could possibly be so cruel! Hands on her hips, she stomped closer. Temper flaring, found she just had to interject, "Excuse me. How is this any different from years ago, when you told my dad that the only way he would ever make MCS the kind of success it could be, was by bringing in total strangers to modernize things?"

He gestured inanely. "It's not."

She slammed her hands on her hips. "Glad we clarified that!"

His tone took on a stony edge. "It was necessary then, Mitzy. Although maybe not in the way I envisioned at that time. It's necessary now."

Mitzy rushed past him. Throwing up her hands, she stalked into the house. "Buck was right about you. Before you got to him, anyway! All you wanted…all you've ever wanted…was my dad's company as another feather in your cap. The fact you weren't able to get it must have really haunted you all these years."

He followed, hard on her heels. "I admit I didn't handle that properly."

She spun around, hands fisted in front of her. "And you think you're doing fine now? Winning over Buck Phillips— who by the way always had your number, at least until now! What did you offer him? Did you hire an architect to renovate his house?"

Chase's lips thinned. "I understand that you're upset. That you don't mean any of these things you are saying."

"You understand nothing!" Mitzy spat back. "But I do!"

Like it or not, she had twenty-nine employees counting on her. She was not going to ruin their Christmas, not for a second year in a row.

"And as much as I am loath to admit it, Chase, the only chance MCS has to survive is in me turning the company over to you." Bitterness clogged her throat. Tears misted her eyes. "I know how you hate to fail so I know you'll take good care of it."

Once again, he did not see where all this was leading. "I'll make Gus proud," he said quietly. "I promise you."

Mitzy was sure he would. Impatient, she stood in the center of the kitchen. "Where are the papers I need to sign?"

He got his briefcase—which was also on the counter.

Took out the contracts that were simultaneously breaking her heart and securing the future. The places were flagged. Here and here, and here and here.

When she was done, she put down her pen. Lifting her chin, she glared at Chase again. "As long as we're having stipulations, I now have one," she told him in her best steel magnolia voice. "I know we're handing out bonuses today, but as for the rest of it, I want to wait until after the New Year before we announce the sale and/or the pending changes to the employees."

"We can't do that," he said. Then added quietly, "Big business doesn't work that way."

Doesn't?

Or won't?

She drew a deep breath. Tried again in her most persuasive voice to raise some empathy in him. "You know how I feel about giving the MCS staff a good holiday this year." Guilt flooded her anew as she admitted with regret, "Especially after what happened last year, when I was too distracted and upset to even realize they were deprived of their annual bonuses." She held out her hands beseechingly. "I want to make it up to them, Chase."

He nodded. Clearly understanding, just not agreeing. "Unfortunately," he said with equal kindness and candor, "this isn't about what I want or what you want, Mitzy. It's about the bottom line." He paused to let his words sink in. "This is business. Not personal."

He was backing her into a corner, the way her mom always pressured her and coerced her into doing things against her better judgment.

She had resisted Judith's machinations for years.

She could resist his.

She let her gaze sift over him. "You own the acquiring corporation, Chase."

He grimaced, to her frustration, digging in all the harder. "Which is the only way I was able to pull this off in such a short amount of time. Plus, get you the bonuses you wanted and the maximum amount of capital to infuse back into MCS, to turn it around."

She knew he had worked wonders on that score. She also knew it wasn't enough. "I appreciate all you have done," Mitzy said carefully, doing her best to preserve what little friendship they had left. "I still don't want to publicly announce any of this until after the New Year."

Exasperation hardened the chiseled lines of his face. "Word like this always gets out, Mitzy. Especially when the staff is already worried and keeping an eagle eye on things."

Mitzy scoffed. "Things like your sudden reappearance in my life, and the inordinate amount of time you've been spending with me?"

"You know why I did that."

Feeling like her whole world was crashing down on her again, she moved closer and locked her eyes with his. "I thought I did."

He let that one pass. Came closer. His jaw clenching, he braced himself as if for battle. "Even if the news of the sale didn't leak, the bonus checks are made out by McCabe Leather Goods. So as soon as they open those envelopes today, the employees will know," he pointed out in a low, lecturing tone. "So it's better we tell them everything up front and answer all their questions."

Was it? Mitzy wondered emotionally.

What if the staff didn't like all the changes? What if they didn't trust any of it? What if this news ruined all of their holidays? There were so many things she had overlooked, hadn't thought to ask, she realized miserably. And all because she had trusted Chase with her entire heart and soul!

Trusted him to ride in like some hunky larger-than-life cowboy, create some big Christmas miracle and save the day.

Whereas he had obviously never lost sight of the end
goal. The end goal he had always had. To make what was
her family's, his.

"Then maybe we should reissue the checks in our current bank's name, so we can do as I originally asked, and
delay the sale announcement until after the New Year."

"And deceive them about what is really going on? That's
not the way I operate, Mitzy. I'm not going to start off with
a lie. I'm going to run the company in a forthright manner from the very start and be as honest with them as I've
been with you, when we make the announcement today."

She stared at him with a mixture of disbelief and shock.
"We." She echoed him through her tears.

"Yes, *we*. Actually…" He took her gently in his arms,
still acting as if he believed he was her conquering hero. "I
was hoping we'd have even more to tell them at the time…"

Hardly able to believe she had spent all that time *making*
him an old-fashioned Christmas present, Mitzy scoffed.
"Like what?" She glanced back at the blueprints he had
showed her. "We're moving in together?"

Even though, she realized with soul-crushing disappointment, there had been no mention of love.

No hope, it seemed, for anything but a hot, passionate affair and a relationship run like a business deal in their future.

"Or getting married," he countered in a calm, cool voice.

Her resolve strengthening, Mitzy could only splay her
hands across his chest and stare. She wanted a love that
surpassed all else, a love that lasted a lifetime. She wanted
their hopes and wishes and dreams to be far more important than any financial bottom line. Because only then
would they have a foundation strong enough to support a
marriage and a family. But clearly Chase did not feel that

way. And never would. "You really thought I would say yes to your cockamamy proposal?"

He recoiled as if she had slapped him. "Given all we've shared the past month? Given how I feel about you and the boys, and you feel about me?" His brow furrowed as she stepped even farther back. "Of course I thought you'd say yes! I thought you'd be happy to say yes!"

Mitzy tried to wrap her mind about what he'd done. "So in other words," she surmised slowly, "you came up with a deal for us, too. I sell you my family company. You give me the bigger house for the quadruplets that I need. In town, where I need to be. And we seal this 'agreement' with what we've both always wanted—at least in theory. A traditional family. Complete with mom, dad and kids."

His lips thinned. "Crudely put, Mitzy," he returned, clearly as insulted as she felt. "But yes, I thought letting go of MCS would be far less painful for you if you got something out of the arrangement that you personally wanted and needed for your long-range happiness, too."

Was he really that naive? That clueless about what made her tick? Apparently so! Mitzy glared at him furiously. "Well, hate to burst your bubble, Chase, but I'm not the only one 'getting fired' today."

Anger flared in his stormy blue eyes. "What do you mean?"

She walked close enough to poke a finger at the hard musculature of his chest. "You, cowboy, are no longer my lover or my friend. Or heaven help us all, a father figure to my boys!" She stepped back and tilted her chin pugnaciously. "Because you might have just saved the company my father left me. But you also destroyed our relationship for the second time! And I will *never ever* forgive you for *any* of this!" Tears blinding her, she strode out.

Chapter Fifteen

December 23

"How are you doing, darling?" Judith asked, late the following afternoon, when Mitzy returned from the grocery store.

Mitzy turned to her mother, grateful Judith and Walter were there a day earlier than planned to celebrate with her and the quads.

Also glad her mother had agreed it would be an intimate family Christmas with just the seven of them, Mitzy set the last of the bags on the counter. "I'm fine."

She walked over to check on the boys. As when she left, all were sleeping soundly in their bassinets.

Judith stepped in to help unload the ingredients for their holiday dinner. "But angry, too."

Mitzy set the onion, sage and celery on the counter. "Can you blame me? After what Chase did at the party yesterday?"

Walter joined them in the kitchen. He stole a bite of the salad her mother was making for that evening's dinner. "I thought the MCS employees were all happy with the buyout announcement and bonus checks."

"They were." Mitzy unloaded the cranberries, oranges and pecans, too. She shook her head. "The worst part is none of them even acted surprised." She picked up the turkey breast and set it in the fridge. "In fact—" much to her chagrin "—they all admitted that they thought Chase would eventually come to the rescue."

"And he did." Judith got up to give the coq au vin a stir.

Mitzy harrumphed, her Christmas spirit entirely gone. Would this day—this season—never end? "While *firing me* and pushing me out of the business entirely in the process!"

Judith put the lid on the skillet. "Surely, you can see it's for the best."

Exhausted down to the marrow, Mitzy sat on a stool at the island. Moaning, she buried her head in her hands. "I promised Dad that I would always take care of the company for him."

Her mother set a mug of mulled cider in front of her. "And you have, by keeping it intact and putting it in the hands of professionals who are cut out to do just that."

Mitzy paused, midsip. "Why is everyone acting as if I was treating it as my little vanity project!"

"Maybe because, if truth be told, you didn't have a clue how to run the venture."

And she hadn't tried to learn, either, until the very end, Mitzy reflected guiltily.

Her mother patted her arm sympathetically. "Your dad tried to talk to you about that before he died, and you wouldn't hear of it for a lot of very understandable reasons."

Grief and fear over the prospect of losing him, being

the major ones, Mitzy thought, beginning to tear up a little again. Darn, if this first Christmas without her dad wasn't every bit as miserable and heartrending as she had expected it would be.

Walter came up on the other side of her. He draped a paternal arm about her shoulders.

"So Gus talked to Chase and together, they put together a fail-safe plan to rescue MCS when the time was right."

Before the end of the fiscal year.

Silence fell.

Mitzy studied her mother. "You don't look as happy about all this as I would have expected."

Judith laid a hand over her heart. "Given how all this broke you and Chase up when the two of you had finally come to your senses and reconciled again? Of course I'm not!"

Glumly, Mitzy stirred her mulled cider with a cinnamon stick. "I know how it looked, Mother, but we weren't re-ally ever together." *Not as anything but friends and lovers.*

"I beg to differ," Walter put in.

Mitzy blinked.

Judith affirmed, "I saw the way you and Chase looked at each other, darling. How wonderful and loving he was with your four babies." She sighed. "I hate to see you lose all that by repeating some of the mistakes I made."

When had her ultraconfident mother become the least bit humble? "What are you talking about?"

Judith poured two more ciders. She and Walter sat opposite Mitzy. "All along, I thought it was the company that was the problem in my marriage to Gus," she admitted gently. "But really it was our attitudes." She paused, regret coming into her eyes. "The fact I resented MCS above all else, and your father revered it above all else. Had either your dad or I been willing to compromise, we would have both been much happier. And in turn, you would have felt more secure, instead of always feeling torn between the two of us."

Mitzy couldn't argue. Much of her childhood had been miserable in that sense, with her never knowing to whom to give her loyalty. Still... "Our situations aren't the same," she argued stubbornly.

Judith put her hand in Walter's. "How do you figure that?"

"You and Dad weren't meant to be. You didn't want the same things. And were never going to. It was the same with your other three husbands, Mother. But with you and Walter...you finally have the wonderful life you always wanted." She paused, close to breaking down in sobs, aware in that moment she had never respected—or needed—her mother more. "Don't you get it? That's what I want. The kind of enduring marriage that the two of you have."

All these years, she'd told herself their marriage was all about money. Now she saw it was so much more.

Her stepfather said, "Don't fool yourself, honey. The life your mother and I have isn't perfect. We still have our differences. But our union is built on a deep enduring love, and we cherish and honor that, and do everything we can to protect our relationship."

Her mother smiled wryly. "We also *compromise* whenever we do find ourselves at odds." Something else her mother had never been inclined to do—before Walter, anyway. But now here she was, giving Mitzy the down-home holiday Mitzy wanted.

That wouldn't have happened before Walter, Mitzy knew.

Mitzy sighed. She looked at Walter. Thought about the way he had turned down her request for a loan in order to preserve his marriage to her mother. He definitely had his priorities in order. "You're saying I should forgive Chase," she guessed slowly.

Walter and Judith exchanged glances. Then Judith said, "We're saying you should think long and hard about what is really important to you, darling. And then act on that."

Chase was outside chopping wood when a familiar pickup truck drove up to the Knotty Pine ranch house. Rachel and Frank emerged, looking ready to school him in a way they hadn't in years. Frank spoke first. "We thought we'd find you here."

Chase centered another log on the stump. Grimly, he split it in two. "You heard?"

His mom folded her arms in front of her. "We were hoping it wasn't true. That Mitzy hadn't broken it off with you."

Chase picked up the pieces and added them to the pile of firewood. "Well, she did. She cast me as the bad guy and blamed me for everything."

Frank moved to better see Chase's face. "Because she didn't like the way the acquisition deal was structured?"

Grimacing, Chase split another log in two. "Because she refuses to understand the way the business world works."

Rachel shivered in the brisk air and motioned to him that she wanted to go inside to finish their conversation.

Reluctantly, he set the blade into the cover.

"That feelings never ever enter into it," Frank guessed.

Chase grabbed a couple of logs. "Right." He escorted them to the ranch house.

"Which is of course why you bent over backward to fulfill a secret promise to Gus," Rachel surmised, as they crossed the threshold.

"Not to mention work the miracles required to save a

company on the verge of bankruptcy, just in time for Christmas," his dad added, taking off his hat and shearling coat.

His mother slipped out of her coat, too. "And threw in a hasty proposal, too."

The way his mom said it made it sound like something he should regret.

"In the vain hope, of course, that Mitzy wouldn't cast you out on your rear," Frank added.

Chase added the logs to the fire he'd been building before deciding he needed to work off a little steam. He tried to tell himself his parents meant well. He lit the match, watched the kindling and rolled-up paper take flame. Then, jaw taut with mounting aggravation, stood. Figuring he was old enough to school them a little, too. "Nice way of putting it, Dad," he drawled.

His sarcasm fell on deaf ears. Frank aimed a thumb at his chest. "Hey, like you, son, I call 'em like I see 'em. And what I see now is a little bit of hypocrisy going on."

"Hypocrisy!" Chase echoed. Him? He strode over to the kitchen sink to wash up. Asked, over his shoulder, "How the heck do you get that?"

His mother followed him, adding with equal disapproval, "Any other deal could have, probably would have, waited, Chase. Until the owners were in such deep distress they had no choice but to sell. Isn't that the way you usually work?" She tilted her head. "Only by the bottom line? So you can maximize your own profit?"

Chase didn't like being made to sound like some kind of Scrooge, with only money on his mind. "Hey! I've ended up saving a lot of companies that way, and making them very successful as part of my conglomerate."

Frank squinted. "That's true," he conceded thoughtfully.

"Then…?" Chase dried his hands.

His father looked him in the eye. "There is a lot more

on the line here than a future of a custom saddle making company."

Rachel touched his arm gently. "We're talking about your future. And Mitzy's. The boys'."

"Mitzy and the quads mean the world to me." Chase's throat grew taut. "But she doesn't want me, Mom." It was as simple and complicated as that.

"Since when have you walked away from something you wanted with all your heart?" his father challenged.

Never—if you didn't consider his broken engagement and broken reconciliation to Mitzy, that was.

Had he given up too soon?

Let his pride stand in the way?

His parents definitely seemed to think so.

"It's not too late to fix things," Rachel advised gently.

His dad nodded. "If anyone can come up with a Christmas miracle, son, it's you…"

Chase thought about his parents' advice the rest of the day and into the night. By morning, he knew what he had to do. A few phone calls later, and the solution was set in motion. Now all he had to do was convince Mitzy to give him another chance.

Deciding to admit he'd screwed up in fashioning a solution without her input, and get down on his knees and beg if he had to, Chase went off to shave and shower. He was dressed in his best sport coat and tie and on his way to the front door, when the bell rang.

Frowning, and hoping it wasn't his family there to give him more unsolicited advice, he went to get it.

Mitzy stood on the other side of the portal. Looking incredibly sexy in heels and a cranberry-red cashmere dress, white wool coat, gloves, and scarf. Was it his imagination? Or was she as nervous as she was determined, just like him? His mouth went dry as he surveyed her. "I was just headed into town to see you."

Her face lit up with a hopeful smile. "Then I'm glad I caught up," she said softly, lifting the "hostess" gift for him to see. She took another quick, tremulous breath. "May I come in?"

Heart pounding, he held the door.

Their fingers brushed as she handed him a holiday basket filled with a bottle of wine and gourmet food. "Courtesy of Judith and Walter. They wanted to thank you for playing Santa at the quadruplets' Dallas debut."

His skin tingling from the brief touch, he thanked her and carried it to the kitchen. "Although, I don't think I did a particularly good job that day."

She peered at him admiringly as she set down her oversize handbag and stripped off her gloves, scarf and coat. "Oh, I think you managed to accomplish quite a lot."

Glad to be focusing on happier memories, he slanted his head, said, "I remember kissing you."

"And I kissed you back."

He felt a catch in his throat. "Mitzy…"

Leaning forward, she pressed a finger to his lips. "I need to talk first, Chase." Her lower lip trembled. "I need to apologize to you. For losing sight of what was really important and thinking the worst of you." Sudden tears glittered. Huskily, she said, "It wasn't your ambition that got in the way this time, it was mine."

Wordlessly, she took him by the hand. When they were settled comfortably on the sofa, she tightened her grasp.

"I thought I could run the company without really doing anything, just because I was Gus's daughter," she said, while he savored the warmth of her slender body snuggled next to his. "When the truth is," she continued, holding on to him like she never wanted to let him go, "like my father, I don't really have a head for the accounting side of business. My dad was an expert craftsman and a people person who excelled in sales, and that carried him and the equally talented people he hired for a long time. But the truth is, MCS was always on the verge of bankruptcy."

"How did you…?"

She drew a breath and continued in a low, tremulous voice, "I had a long talk with Buck Phillips and some of the other employees after the party wrapped up. It turns out they've been worried for years that one day the company would just flame out."

He let out his breath slowly, glad she finally recognized the hard truth. And didn't fault him for seeing it, too.

Mitzy's soft lips twisted into a rueful smile. "Or as Walter says, it's not enough to just have talent. You have to know how to harness it. I don't. You do. And because of you, Chase, and all the hard work you've done, everyone who worked for my dad over the years will continue to have jobs."

He looked deep into her eyes, determined to do whatever he needed to, to make this right. "I'm glad you understand that," he said quietly, aware he needed a lot more out of their relationship than they'd had. He sensed she did, too. "But you're not the only one who made a huge mistake, Mitzy."

He shook his head in regret. "I was equally blind to think that emotion never has any part in business. In any successful organization, loyalty, a passion for excellence and a love of what everyone is doing plays a huge part. MCS has that in spades," he told her hoarsely, shifting her onto his lap. Knowing that even though the company her father had founded had torn them apart—twice—it was also bringing them back together again.

He stroked a hand through her hair. "And your familial

connection to the company is as much an integral part of the MCS legacy as Gus's memory."

She swallowed but her gaze didn't waver. "So what are you saying?" she asked, confused. "You regret buying MCS? Firing me?" She shifted toward him, a pulse throbbing in her throat. "Because I have to tell you, in retrospect I think you were completely right to do both. It's a relief not to have the weight of the company on my shoulders. To know it's in good hands. That everyone who works there is going to be just fine."

He nodded, understanding. "I still regret structuring the deal the way I did. I knew how much Gus's legacy meant to you, that MCS was a connection to him, and I didn't take that into consideration as much as I should have. Which is why I've taken steps to make amends, too."

She settled more intimately against him, curving one hand over his shoulder, placing the other over his heart. "How?"

He grinned, happy to admit, "I bought out all the other shares of MCS. I'm putting it in trust, so it'll always carry Gus's name and be there for you and your kids."

Mitzy blinked. "All of it?"

"The entire company."

Her soft breasts lifted as she jerked in a surprised breath. "That's one hell of a gift, cowboy."

He slanted her a comically provoking look. "Well, I guess it doesn't hurt to admit," he confessed wryly, teasing, "there are a few strings…"

"Now this sounds like the wheeling and dealing Chase McCabe I know."

He sobered. "You have to give me another chance to make things right between us, too."

"I already have. It's why I came out here today. Because…"

She went over to her oversize handbag and pulled out two gaily wrapped presents.

The first contained an old-fashioned scrapbook bearing the title "Mitzy and Chase, The Beginning," and was jammed with all the mementos of their past.

Hope swelled in his heart. Thinking this could only mean one thing, that she was ready to give them a second chance to remedy the foolishness of their original breakup, he said, "You're giving this to me?"

She hitched in a breath. "I thought we'd share it." Her smile meshed with his. "Along with…" She handed him the smaller gift. Beneath the paper was a familiar velvet jewelry box that brought up a new wealth of emotion.

She swallowed, determined, it seemed, to own up to and fix every mistake the two of them had made.

"I'm calling off the end of our engagement. And asking…" Lower lip trembling, she slid off his lap and dropped to her knees. "No, begging…you to let us go back to the point where everything began to go wrong…and let us pick up…and go from there."

Aware it was all about to work out the way they'd both always wished, he got down on his knees beside her, prepared to completely humble himself, too.

"You want to get married?" he rasped.

She gripped his biceps, then hugged him fiercely, ready to be vulnerable in a way she never had been before. "As soon as possible."

They kissed, sweetly and tenderly.

Gallantly, he stood and helped her to her feet.

"So, if you say yes—" she opened up the ring box to reveal the diamond solitaire he had given her years before "—I'll put this back on my finger."

"Nothing would make me happier, darlin'." Chase took

it from her and proudly did the honors. It was as it had been before, a perfect fit. And a portent of their future.

"And we can start sending out the invitations…" Mitzy said giddily, holding out her hand to admire the glittering stone.

He caught her by the waist and tugged her close. "This is quite a Christmas gift!"

Mitzy wreathed her arms about his neck and tilted her face up to his, all the love he had ever wanted to see reflected in her pretty eyes. She whispered affectionately, "I love you, Chase. I've always loved you…"

Talk about every Christmas wish he'd ever had coming true! "I've always loved you, too, sweetheart," he murmured hoarsely. "And I always will." He lowered his head and they kissed again.

"So it's official? We're on again?" Mitzy asked, at long last.

Feeling like he'd finally come home, Chase brushed his lips across her temple, her cheek, her ear. "You bet we're on." He found his way to her lips once again. "It's time we started living our lives the way they were meant to be lived— together—as husband and wife!" He tunneled his hands through her hair and captured her lips in another ardent kiss.

She kissed him back deeply, holding fast, finally prepared to let down her guard and take that final leap of faith with him. "And speaking of holiday miracles…!" she teased softly.

Chase wrapped his arms about her. "Looks like we found ours, after all."

She flashed the enticing smile he adored. "You're right about that, cowboy," she murmured contentedly. "This is shaping up to be the Best. Christmas. Ever."

Epilogue

"So this is what an at-home elopement looks like," Mitzy murmured happily, six days later, after the vows had been said and congratulations were being made.

Thanks to her mother's hard work, the home she had inherited from her father had been transformed into a winter wonderland, the holiday decorations supplanted with garlands of cream roses, pale pink orchids and baby's breath. The beautifully decked-out fireplace mantel was serving as the altar. Their immediate families and the quadruplets were all gathered around.

Chase winked. "We're lucky your mom is such a pro at pulling together social gatherings."

Judith hugged them both. "Actually, I think we're lucky you and Chase found each other again after all these years."

"Which maybe," Walter added kindly, "was Gus's plan in asking Chase to come in and save the day."

Which he had done.

The family company was safe, Gus's legacy protected, the burden of trying to do a job that was out of her depth while simultaneously caring for infant quadruplets, removed.

"You're going to have to take Chase up on renovating that new home for you, though," Judith murmured. "If he works at home at all this place won't be big enough for the six of you for long."

Rachel said, "Or you can always move out to his ranch and expand that later. If you decide living in the country is what you want."

"What's important," Frank added, "is family, and being together."

"Hear, hear to that." Walter raised a glass.

Toasts followed.

One after another.

Finally, Mitzy and Chase left on their honeymoon, which was going to be conducted at the Knotty Pines Ranch. As they drove down the lane to the ranch house, Chase slanted her a glance and asked, "Worried about being away from the boys?"

Mitzy waited for him to circle around and help her with the door. As he did so, she couldn't help but admire how devastatingly handsome he looked in his dark suit and tie.

The skirt of her cream-colored satin suit rode up slightly as she stepped out and onto the ground. She slid her arm through his. Together, they walked toward the house. "It's only one night, and the boys have four grandparents, who are well acquainted with their routine, taking care of them in a very familiar place," Mitzy reminded drily. "I think they'll be okay."

Chase paused only long enough to unlock the door. "What about us?" He swung her up into his arms and carried her across the threshold.

Inside, the Christmas tree lights were on, a fire had been lit and a private late-night supper awaited them.

He set her down. Gathered her close and tilted her face up to his. "Are we going to be okay?"

Knowing her happiness was as important to him as his was to her, Mitzy nodded confidently. She wound her arms about his neck. "More than okay, given that we're finally together the way we were always meant to be. And have the family we always wanted, too."

He grinned, vowing softly, "No more wasting time, sweetheart. From here on out, we're going to cherish and hold on to every incredible moment."

Mitzy nodded, even as the lump in her throat grew. The happily-ever-after she had always hoped for was finally happening. "You know I love you with all my heart and soul," she whispered fiercely.

"And I love you more than I ever thought humanly possible."

Mitzy rose up on tiptoe, pressing her body against the solid warmth of his. She kissed him sweetly. Once, and then again. And again. "To our future, then?" she proposed.

Chase nodded joyfully and kissed her back, just as reverently. "Which starts right now."

* * * * *

Please watch for the
next book in Cathy Gillen Thacker's
Texas Legends: The Mccabes miniseries,
coming April 2019, only from
Harlequin Special Edition!

Turn the page for a sneak peek at
New York Times *bestselling author*
RaeAnne Thayne's next heartwarming
Haven Point romance,
Season of Wonder,
available October 2018
from HQN Books!

Dani Capelli and her daughters are facing
their first Christmas in Haven Point.
But Ruben Morales—the son of Dani's new boss—
is determined to give them a season of wonder!

CHAPTER ONE

"This is totally lame. Why do we have to stay here and wait for you? We can walk home in, like, ten minutes."

Daniela Capelli drew in a deep breath and prayed for patience, something she seemed to be doing with increasing frequency these days when it came to her thirteen-year-old daughter. "It's starting to snow and already almost dark."

Silver rolled her eyes, something *she* did with increasing frequency these days. "So what? A little snow won't kill us. I would hardly even call that snow. We had way bigger storms than this back in Boston. Remember that big blizzard a few years ago, when school was closed for, like, a week?"

"I remember," her younger daughter, Mia, said, looking up from her coloring book at Dani's desk at the Haven Point Veterinary Clinic. "I stayed home from preschool and I watched Anna and Elsa a thousand times, until you said your eardrums would explode if I played it one more time."

Dani could hear a bark from the front office that likely signaled the arrival of her next client and knew she didn't have time to stand here arguing with an obstinate teenager.

"Mia can't walk as fast as you can. You'll end up frustrated with her and you'll both be freezing before you make it home," she pointed out.

"So she can stay here and wait for you while I walk home. I just told Chelsea we could FaceTime about the new dress she bought and she can only do it for another hour before her dad comes to pick her up for his visitation."

"Why can't you FaceTime here? I only have two more patients to see. I'll be done in less than an hour, then we can all go home together. You can hang out in the waiting room with Mia, where the Wi-Fi signal is better."

Silver gave a huge put-upon sigh but picked up her backpack and stalked out of Dani's office toward the waiting room.

"Can I turn on the TV out there?" Mia asked as she gathered her papers and crayons. "I like the dog shows."

The veterinary clinic showed calming clips of animals on a big flat-screen TV set low to the ground for their clientele.

"After Silver's done with her phone call, okay?"

"She'll take *forever*," Mia predicted with a gloomy look. "She always does when she's talking to Chelsea."

Dani fought to hide a smile. "Thanks for your patience, sweetie, with her and with me. Finish your math worksheet while you're here, then when we get home, you can watch what you want."

Both the Haven Point elementary and middle schools were within walking distance of the clinic and it had become a habit for Silver to walk to the elementary school and then walk with Mia to the clinic to spend a few hours until they could all go home together.

Of late, Silver had started to complain that she didn't want to pick her sister up at the elementary school every day, that she would rather they both just took their respective school buses home, where Silver could watch her sister without having to hang out at the boring veterinary clinic.

This working professional/single mother gig was *hard*, she thought as she ushered Mia to the waiting room. Then again, in most ways it was much easier than the veterinary student/single mother gig had been.

When they entered the comfortable waiting room— with its bright colors, pet-friendly benches and big fish tank—Mia faltered for a moment, then sidestepped behind Dani's back.

She saw instantly what had caused her daughter's nervous reaction. Funny. Dani felt the same way. She wanted to hide behind somebody, too.

The receptionist had given her the files with the dogs' names that were coming in for a checkup but hadn't mentioned their human was Ruben Morales. Her gorgeous next-door neighbor.

Dani's palms instantly itched and her stomach felt as if she'd accidentally swallowed a flock of butterflies.

"Deputy Morales," she said, then paused, hating the slightly breathless note in her voice.

What *was* it about the man that always made her so freaking nervous?

He was big, yes, at least six feet tall, with wide shoulders, tough muscles and a firm, don't-mess-with-me jawline.

It wasn't just that. Even without his uniform, the man exuded authority and power, which instantly raised her hackles and left her uneasy, something she found both frustrating and annoying about herself.

No matter how far she had come, how hard she had

worked to make a life for her and her girls, she still sometimes felt like the troublesome foster kid from Queens.

She had done her best to avoid him in the months they
had been in Haven Point, but that was next to impossible
when they lived so close to each other—and when she was
the intern in his father's veterinary practice.

"Hey, Doc," he said, flashing her an easy smile she
didn't trust for a moment. It never quite reached his dark,
long-lashed eyes, at least where she was concerned.

While she might be uncomfortable around Ruben Morales, his dogs were another story.

He held the leashes of both of them, a big, muscular Bel-
gian shepherd and an incongruously paired little Chi-poo,
and she reached down to pet both of them. They sniffed
her and wagged happily, the big dog's tail nearly knock-
ing over his small friend.

That was the thing she loved most about dogs. They
were uncomplicated and generous with their affection, for
the most part. They never looked at people with that subtle
hint of suspicion, as if trying to uncover all their secrets.

"I wasn't expecting you," she admitted.

"Oh? I made an appointment. The boys both need
checkups. Yukon needs his regular hip and eye check and
Ollie is due for his shots."

She gave the dogs one more pat before she straightened
and faced him, hoping his sharp cop eyes couldn't notice
evidence of her accelerated pulse.

"Your father is still here every Monday and Friday af-
ternoons. Maybe you should reschedule with him," she
suggested. It was a faint hope, but a girl had to try.

"Why would I do that?"

"Maybe because he's your father and knows your dogs?"

"Dad is an excellent veterinarian. Agreed. But he's also
semiretired and wants to be fully retired this time next

year. As long as you plan to stick around in Haven Point, we will have to switch vets and start seeing you eventually. I figured we might as well start now."

He was checking her out. Not *her* her, but her skills as a veterinarian.

The implication was clear. She had been here three months, and it had become obvious during that time in their few interactions that Ruben Morales was extremely protective of his family. He had been polite enough when they had met previously, but always with a certain guardedness, as if he was afraid she planned to take the good name his hardworking father had built up over the years for the Haven Point Veterinary Clinic and drag it through the sludge at the bottom of Lake Haven.

Dani pushed away her instinctive prickly defensiveness, bred out of all those years in foster care when she felt as if she had no one else to count on—compounded by the difficult years after she married Tommy and had Silver, when she *really* had no one else in her corner.

She couldn't afford to offend Ruben. She didn't need his protective wariness to turn into full-on suspicion. With a little digging, Ruben could uncover things about her and her past that would ruin everything for her and her girls here.

She forced a professional smile. "It doesn't matter. Let's go back to a room and take a look at these guys. Girls, I'll be done shortly. Silver, keep an eye on your sister."

Her oldest nodded without looking up from her phone and with an inward sigh, Dani led the way to the largest of the exam rooms.

She stood at the door as he entered the room with the two dogs, then joined him inside and closed it behind her.

The large room seemed to shrink unnaturally and she paused inside for a moment, flustered and wishing she could escape. Dani gave herself a mental shake. She could handle being in the same room with the one man in Haven Point who left her breathless and unsteady.

All she had to do was focus on the reason he was here in the first place. His dogs.

She knelt to their level. "Hey there, guys. Who wants to go first?"

The Malinois wagged his tail again while his smaller counterpoint sniffed around her shoes, probably picking up the scents of all the other dogs she had seen that day.

"Ollie, I guess you're the winner today."

He yipped, his big ears that stuck straight out from his face quivering with excitement.

He was the funniest-looking dog, quirky and unique, with wisps of fur in odd places, spindly legs and a narrow Chihuahua face. She found him unbearably cute. With that face, she wouldn't ever be able to say no to him if he were hers.

"Can I give him a treat?" She always tried to ask permission first from her clients' humans.

"Only if you want him to be your best friend for life," Ruben said.

Despite her nerves, his deadpan voice sparked a smile, which widened when she gave the little dog one of the treats she always carried in the pocket of her lab coat. He slurped it up in one bite, then sat with a resigned sort of patience during the examination.

She was aware of Ruben watching her as she carefully examined the dog, but Dani did her best not to let his scrutiny fluster her.

She knew what she was doing, she reminded herself. She had worked so hard to be here, sacrificing all her time, energy and resources of the last decade to nothing else but her girls and her studies.

"Everything looks good," she said after checking out the dog and finding nothing unusual. "He seems like a healthy little guy. It says here he's about six or seven. So you haven't had him from birth?"

"No. Only about two years. He was a stray I picked up off the side of the road between here and Shelter Springs when I was on patrol one day. He was in a bad way, half-starved, fur matted. As small as he is, it's a wonder he wasn't picked off by a coyote or even one of the bigger hawks. He just needed a little TLC."

"You couldn't find his owner?"

"We ran ads and Dad checked with all his contacts at shelters and veterinary clinics from here to Boise with no luck. I had been fostering him while we looked, and to be honest, I kind of lost my heart to the little guy, and by then Yukon adored him so we decided to keep him."

She was such a sucker for animal lovers, especially those who rescued the vulnerable and lost ones.

And, no, she didn't need counseling to point out the parallels to her own life.

Regardless, she couldn't let herself be drawn to Ruben and risk doing something foolish. She had too much to lose here in Haven Point.

"What about Yukon here?" She knelt down to examine the bigger dog. In her experience, sometimes bigger dogs didn't like to be lifted and she wasn't sure if the beautiful Malinois fell into that category.

Ruben shrugged as he scooped Ollie onto his lap to keep the little Chi-poo from swooping in and stealing the treat she held out for the bigger dog. "You could say he was a rescue, too."

"Oh?"

"He was a K-9 officer down in Mountain Home. After his handler was killed in the line of duty, I guess he kind of went into a canine version of depression and wouldn't work with anyone else. I know that probably sounds crazy."

She scratched the dog's ears, touched by the bond that could build between handler and dog. "Not at all," she said briskly. "I've seen many dogs go into decline when their owners die. It's not uncommon."

"For a year or so, they tried to match him up with other officers, but things never quite gelled, for one reason or another, then his eyes started going. His previous handler who died was a good buddy of mine from the academy, and I couldn't let him go just anywhere."

"Retired police dogs don't always do well in civilian life. They can be aggressive with other dogs and sometimes people. Have you had any problems with that?"

"Not with Yukon. He's friendly. Aren't you, buddy? You're a good boy."

Dani could swear the dog grinned at his owner, his tongue lolling out.

Yukon was patient while she looked him over, especially as she maintained a steady supply of treats.

When she finished, she gave the dog a pat and stood. "Can I take a look at Ollie's ears one more time?"

"Sure. Help yourself."

He held the dog out and she reached for Ollie. As she did, the dog wriggled a little, and Dani's hands ended up brushing Ruben's chest. She froze at the accidental contact, a shiver rippling down her spine. She pinned her reaction on the undeniable fact that it had been entirely too long since she had touched a man, even accidentally.

She had to cut out this *fascination* or whatever it was immediately. Clean-cut, muscular cops were *not* her type, and the sooner she remembered that the better.

She focused on checking the ears of the little dog, gave him one more scratch and handed him back to Ruben.

"That should do it. A clean bill of health. You obviously take good care of them."

He patted both dogs with an affectionate smile that did nothing to ease her nerves.

"My dad taught me well. I spent most of my youth helping out here at the clinic—cleaning cages, brushing coats, walking the occasional overnight boarder. Whatever grunt work he needed. He made all of us help."

"I can think of worse ways to earn a dime," she said.

The chance to work with animals would have been a dream opportunity for her, back when she had few bright spots in her world.

"So can I. I always loved animals."

She had to wonder why he didn't follow in his father's footsteps and become a vet. If he had, she probably wouldn't be here right now, as Frank Morales probably would have handed down his thriving practice to his own progeny.

Not that it was any of her business. Ruben certainly could follow any career path he wanted—as long as that path took him far away from her.

"Give me a moment to grab those medications and I'll be right back."

"No rush."

Out in the hall, she closed the door behind her and drew in a deep breath.

Get a grip, she chided herself. *He's just a hot-looking dude. Heaven knows you've had more than enough experience with those to last a lifetime.*

She went to the well-stocked medication dispensary, found what she needed and returned to the exam room.

Outside the door, she paused for only a moment to gather her composure before pushing it open. "Here are the pills for Ollie's nerves and a refill for Yukon's eyedrops," she said briskly. "Let me know if you have any questions—though if you do, you can certainly ask your father."

"Thanks." As he took them from her, his hands brushed hers again and sent a little spark of awareness shivering through her.

She was probably imagining the way his gaze sharpened, as if he had felt something odd, too.

"I can show you out. We're shorthanded today since the veterinary tech and the receptionist both needed to leave early."

"No problem. That's what I get for scheduling the last appointment of the day—though, again, I spent most of my youth here. I think we can find our way."

"It's fine. I'll show you out." She stood outside the door while he gathered the dogs' leashes, then led the way toward the front office.

After three months, Ruben still couldn't get a bead on Dr. Daniela Capelli.

His next-door neighbor still seemed a complete enigma to him. By all reports from his father, she was a dedicated, earnest new veterinarian with a knack for solving difficult medical mysteries and a willingness to work hard. She seemed like a warm and loving mother, at least from the few times he had seen her interactions with her two girls, the uniquely named teenager Silver—who had, paradoxically, purple hair—and the sweet-as-Christmas-toffee Mia, who was probably about six.

He also couldn't deny she was beautiful, with slender features, striking green eyes, dark, glossy hair and a dusky skin tone that proclaimed her Italian heritage—as if her name didn't do the trick first.

He actually liked the trace of New York accent that

slipped into her speech at times. It fitted her somehow, in a way he couldn't explain. Despite that, he couldn't deny that the few times he had interacted with more than a wave in passing, she was brusque, prickly and sometimes downright distant.

His father adored her and wouldn't listen to a negative thing about her.

You just have to get to know her, Frank had said the other night. He apparently didn't see how diligently Dani Capelli worked to keep anyone else from doing just that.

She wasn't unfriendly, only distant. She kept herself to herself. Did Dani have any idea how fascinated the people of Haven Point were with these new arrivals in their midst?

Or maybe that was just him.

As he followed her down the hall in her white lab coat, his dogs behaving themselves for once, Ruben told himself to forget about his stupid attraction to her.

When they walked into the clinic waiting room, they found her two girls there. The older one was texting on her phone while her sister did somersaults around the room.

Dani stopped in the doorway and seemed to swallow an exasperated sound. "Mia, honey, you're going to have dog hair all over you."

"I'm a snowball rolling down the hill," the girl said. "Can't you see me getting bigger and bigger and bigger?"

He could tell the moment the little girl spotted him and his dogs coming into the area behind her mother. She went still and then slowly rose to her feet, features shifting from gleeful to nervous.

Why was she so afraid of him?

"You make a very good snowball," he said, pitching his voice low and calm as his father had taught him to do with all skittish creatures. "I haven't seen anybody somersault that well in a long time."

She moved to her mother's side and buried her face in Dani's white coat—though he didn't miss the way she reached down to pet Ollie on her way.

"Hey again, Silver."

He knew the older girl from the middle school, where he served as the resource officer a few hours a week. He made it a point to learn all the students' names and tried to talk to them individually when he had the chance, in hopes that if they had a problem they would feel comfortable coming to him.

He had the impression that Silver was like her mother in many ways. Reserved, wary, slow to trust. It made him wonder just who had hurt them.

Don't miss Season of Wonder
by RaeAnne Thayne,
available October 2018
wherever HQN books and ebooks are sold!

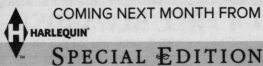

COMING NEXT MONTH FROM

HARLEQUIN®

SPECIAL EDITION

Available October 16, 2018

#2653 THE MAVERICK'S CHRISTMAS TO REMEMBER
Montana Mavericks: The Lonelyhearts Ranch • by Christy Jeffries
Wedding planner Caroline Ruth comes to after a fall off a ladder believing
she's engaged to Craig Clifton—but they've never met before! The doctors
don't want Caroline getting too upset, so Craig goes along with the charade.
But what's a cowboy to do when his fake feelings turn real?

#2654 THE MAJORS' HOLIDAY HIDEAWAY
American Heroes • by Caro Carson
Major India Woods thought house-sitting in Texas would be just another
globe-trotting adventure—until her friend's neighbor, Major Aidan Nord,
shows up. But their hot holiday fling is interrupted by his two little girls, and
India thinks she might have just found her most exciting adventure yet!

#2655 A STONECREEK CHRISTMAS REUNION
Maggie & Griffin • by Michelle Major
Griffin Stone is back in town, this time with a little boy in tow! Can Maggie
forgive his disappearing act? And will Stonecreek win over a tech CEO to
host their new headquarters? Find out in the anticipated third book of the
Maggie & Griffin trilogy!

#2656 AN UNEXPECTED CHRISTMAS BABY
The Daycare Chronicles • by Tara Taylor Quinn
Tamara Owens is supposed to be finding whoever has been stealing from
her father's company. But when she meets prime suspect Flint Collins—and
his new charge, infant Diamond—she can't bear to pull away, despite her
tragic past. Will Flint be able to look past her original investigation to make
them a family by Christmas?

#2657 WYOMING CHRISTMAS SURPRISE
The Wyoming Multiples • by Melissa Senate
Moments before walking down the aisle again, Allie Stark finds her
presumed-dead husband at her door. Little does he know, he became the
father of four babies in his absence! Can this reunited couple make their
family work the second time around?

#2658 THE SERGEANT'S CHRISTMAS MISSION
The Brands of Montana • by Joanna Sims
Former army sergeant Shane Brand's life has stalled. When his new landlady,
the lovely Rebecca Adams, and her two children move in, he finds he's
suddenly ready to change. Now it's his new mission to be the man the single
mom deserves, in time to give them all a dose of Christmas joy.

**YOU CAN FIND MORE INFORMATION ON UPCOMING HARLEQUIN® TITLES,
FREE EXCERPTS AND MORE AT WWW.HARLEQUIN.COM.**

HSECNM1018

Tamara Owens is supposed to be finding the person stealing from her father. But when she meets prime suspect Flint Collins—and his new charge, Diamond— she can't bear to pull away, despite her tragic past. Will Flint be able to look past her lies to make them a family by Christmas?

Read on for a sneak preview of the next book in The Daycare Chronicles,
An Unexpected Christmas Baby
by USA TODAY bestselling author Tara Taylor Quinn.

How hadn't he heard her first knock?

And then she saw the carrier on the chair next to him. He'd been rocking it.

"What on earth are you doing to that baby?" she exclaimed, nothing in mind but to rescue the child in obvious distress.

"Damned if I know," he said loudly enough to be heard over the noise. "I fed her, burped her, changed her. I've done everything they said to do, but she won't stop crying."

Tamara was already unbuckling the strap that held the crying infant in her seat. She was so tiny! Couldn't have been more than a few days old. There were no tears on her cheeks.

"There's nothing poking her. I checked," Collins said, not interfering as she lifted the baby from the seat, careful to support the little head.

It wasn't until that warm weight settled against her that Tamara realized what she'd done. She was holding a baby. Something she couldn't do.

She was going to pay. With a hellacious nightmare at the very least.

The baby's cries had stopped as soon as Tamara picked her up.

"What did you do?" Collins was there, practically touching her, he was standing so close.

"Nothing. I picked her up."

"There must've been some problem with the seat, after all…" He'd tossed the infant head support on the desk and was removing the washable cover.

"I'm guessing she just wanted to be held," Tamara said. What the hell was she doing?

Tearless crying generally meant anger, not physical distress. And why did Flint Collins have a baby in his office?

She had to put the child down. But couldn't until he put the seat back together. The newborn's eyes were closed and she hiccuped and then sighed.

Clenching her lips for a second, Tamara looked away. "Babies need to be held almost as much as they need to be fed," she told him while she tried to understand what was going on.

He was checking the foam beneath the seat cover and the straps, too. He was fairly distraught himself.

Not what she would've predicted from a hard-core businessman possibly stealing from her father.

"Who is she?" she asked, figuring it was best to start at the bottom and work her way up to exposing him for the thief he probably was.

He straightened. Stared at the baby in her arms, his brown eyes softening and yet giving away a hint of what looked like fear at the same time. In that second she wished like hell that her father was wrong and Collins wouldn't turn out to be the one who was stealing from Owens Investments.

Don't miss
An Unexpected Christmas Baby *by Tara Taylor Quinn,*
available November 2018 wherever
Harlequin® Special Edition books and ebooks are sold.

www.Harlequin.com

Looking for more satisfying love stories
with community and family at their core?

Check out **Harlequin® Special Edition**
and **Love Inspired®** books!

New books available every month!

CONNECT WITH US AT:

Facebook.com/groups/HarlequinConnection

Facebook.com/HarlequinBooks

Twitter.com/HarlequinBooks

Instagram.com/HarlequinBooks

Pinterest.com/HarlequinBooks

ReaderService.com

**ROMANCE WHEN
YOU NEED IT**

HFGENRE2018

Need an adrenaline rush from nail-biting tales
(and irresistible males)?

Check out **Harlequin Intrigue®**
and **Harlequin® Romantic Suspense** books!

New books available every month!

CONNECT WITH US AT:

Facebook.com/groups/HarlequinConnection

Facebook.com/HarlequinBooks

Twitter.com/HarlequinBooks

Instagram.com/HarlequinBooks

Pinterest.com/HarlequinBooks

ReaderService.com

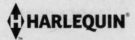

**ROMANCE WHEN
YOU NEED IT**

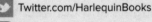
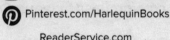

Love Harlequin romance?

DISCOVER.

Be the first to find out about promotions,
news and exclusive content!

Facebook.com/HarlequinBooks

Twitter.com/HarlequinBooks

Instagram.com/HarlequinBooks

Pinterest.com/HarlequinBooks

ReaderService.com

EXPLORE.

Sign up for the Harlequin e-newsletter and
download a free book from any series at
TryHarlequin.com.

CONNECT.

Join our Harlequin community to share
your thoughts and connect with other
romance readers!
Facebook.com/groups/HarlequinConnection

HARLEQUIN®

**ROMANCE WHEN
YOU NEED IT**

HSOCIAL2018